Other titles by the author

Movin' On
Continuin' On
Ramblin' On
Moon over Manila
Hawaiian Paniolo
Sitting on a Goldmine
Floater on the Reef
Christmas in the Tropics
The Korean Shadow (children)
Shrimp: The Way You Like It
The Royal Headley of Pohnpei
Adios Muchacho—Burn in Hell
Stories from Wild Bill's Café (Anthology)
The Mystery Hotel

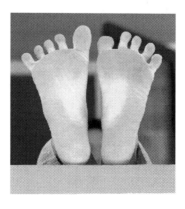

The Mystery Hotel

Come for a Rest...or to Die

JOE RACE

Order this book online at www.trafford.com
or email orders@trafford.com
Most Trafford titles are also available at major online book retailers.

Author's photo by Paila Miradora, Dobie Zeus photo by Bud White

Printed in the United States of America.

ISBN: 978-1-4669-1425-4 (sc)
ISBN: 978-1-4669-1426-1 (e)

Library of Congress Control Number: 2012902713

Trafford rev. 02/28/2012

www.trafford.com

North America & international
toll-free: 1 888 232 4444 (USA & Canada)
phone: 250 383 6864 • fax: 812 355 4082

To all the **Grandpa and Granny Boote Kids,**
spread far and wide on the planet,
and it all started in the flower gardens of the U.K.

Japanese saying:

*Traveler, pray lodge in this unworthy house. The bath is ready.
A peaceful room awaits you. Come in! Come in!*

—Translation of a sign at the doorway of a *minshuku/ryokan*,
Kyoto, Japan

Contents

Acknowledgements

Once again, it is time to thank all my fearless, never-hesitating supporters during the concept, birth and climax of this island story: Salve' and the Race Kids—Jeff, Jim, Cindy, Lynnie, Sylvia, Yoshi, Nobu, Kimi, Gresil, Paila and George. And of course, Urbano, Russ, Bill, Ulan, Dan, Ron, John, Bud, Donna, Franko, Tony, Mary, Katrina, Connie, Jane and many others. Mahalo also to my loyal audience who snap up the books either in soft cover or E-format—you folks keep the *ohana* family supplied with rice and chicken . . . and Starbuck coffee. Stay focused and happy, and when you get a wee bit depressed, grab your canoe and paddle out to the island life. See you on the next tropical adventure!

Also, A Special Thanks to my English students at Northern Marianas College who helped me brainstorm the plot for this novel: Jason Arriola. Sang Woo Han, Escoanne Hocog, Alvin Indalecio, Jeric Maglonzo, Nicolas Nekai, Yuri No, Hee Sun Ohng, Rosario Peter, Leoric Primo, Rachelle Rivera, Christine Sablan, Jonica Taisacan, Mark Yebra, Augustin Aguon, Rosher Apolinar, Bolo Cabrera, Gregory Deleon Guerrero, Jessica Deleon Guerrero, Davenalt Jones, Cecil Kapileo, Matsuda Kloulechad, Joselito Pena, Lea Santiago, Kayla Santos, April Villocino, Fiona William, and Shanalyn William. We put the brainstorming and cluster processes to good use. You were great!

THE MYSTERY HOTEL
Come for a Rest…or to Die

Introduction

A hotel is a lodging where you can go and rest, stay in comfort and safety when you're away from home for its necessary amenities, or just take a respite from the daily grind of life in the basic urban setting. Saipan has such a hotel—at very practical, reasonable rates, and it sits on a bluff overlooking the Philippine Sea. It's a great hotel for photography and beachcombing—and romance. A long sandy beach is right below the hotel. A guest just takes a 92-step native-stone stairway down to the water, and *voila*, you're on a near-private beach. If you like to go *au naturale*, there are several little coves where you can hide out.

There's also a mini-marina on the north end of the property, which can accommodate all vessels from small fishing boats to noisy speed-boats, and luxurious yachts from around the world. Even the Navy Seals in training popped up on the dock one night during the darkest new moon.

You can also hitch a ride in a red jeep on a round-about dirt road. There are chairs and tables on the sandy beach to suit every size—and constructed of bamboo and mangrove wood. There is a palm frond *utt* (four posts and a roof) for shade and an electrical outlet for your favorite CD. The posts are lined with coconut husks, all sprouting with air-borne orchids of numerous colors from far-away lands.

If you let your mind wander, you realize that you can go strolling on the white sand where generations of Chamorro and Carolinian peoples have walked and searched for food, and made love. Pick up a flat rock and skip it across the lagoon—that same rock has likely been thrown a hundred times.

The hotel is officially called *"The Californian,"* based on the name of a mystical land from the Spanish novel *Las Sergas de Esplandian* by Garcia Ordonez de Montalvo. Some of the words in the novel are posted on the walls of the spacious library, in both English and Spanish. The architecture of the three buildings is very much like the old cities of Spain with their red-tiled roofs and stuccoed walls. There is usually no need for air-conditioning because of soft ocean breezes and lush trees that hang over the roofs to keep the bedrooms cool. By observation and feel, it is a very peaceful, serene place to stay. It is nothing less than a splendid paradise.

The hotel gets all types of guests: honeymooners, lost souls, wanderers, vacationers, writers, researchers, divers, and a variety of gangsters, crooked politicians, and outlaws (they also need rest and a chance to recharge the batteries). Sometimes the prosties that service other hotels check in during their monthlies and just lie around the pool and read a good book. They turn off their cell phones.

The "Golden Weeks" of China and Japan are culturally refreshing and help to make the financial books solid. Both countries tie a number of holidays together so that the workers get up to a week off at one time. Often the home countries and employers pick up the tab to help the employees relax and relieve stress. China's Golden Week happens twice a year—the Spring Festival during January or February and then a National Week in October. Japan's Golden Week is in late May celebrating the birth of Emperor Satowa and the "greening" of the country.

The hotel center building is the office and computer terminals (available to guests), and also houses the 5-star restaurant. It also hosts the gym, pool entry and massage tables. The pool is bright blue and is Olympic size for guests serious about swimming and diving. There is a smoking room for the Asian guests to enjoy, and for the cigar aficionados. The finest international smokes and accruements are available. The building right on the bluff is for long-term guests, people that own businesses on the island or are simply retired. The building towards the east is for short-term guests, and travelers that are staying for up to four weeks. It is also the section for hourly guests and has covered parking for privacy, out of sight of the island residents and patrons of the restaurant. There are a total of eighty rooms and six exclusive penthouse suites. There is a clear view of the ocean from every room, except of course, from the well-stocked wine cellar.

As in any business venture, there are variables. At night, the hotel can become eerie, almost frightening, when the wind blows hard and there are numerous power outages. Things are not always as they seem all the time.

The locals call it "The Mystery Hotel" for obvious good reasons. There are many secrets and unusual happenings at the hotel, some of which have involved murder and strange disappearances of guests and hotel workers. They are many torrid tales. Workers have reported seeing spooks, witches, hobgoblins, *mangkukulams* (hovering ghosts) and *tao-taomonas* (jungle creatures) flying across the property and especially in the hallways. Imaginations have run wild. Sometimes it almost impossible to hire superstitious employees—many are afraid to work at the hotel. Weird noises have been heard from the bedrooms. No one quite knew how to specifically describe the noises except as haunting and inhuman, or maybe biologically a woman reaching ecstasy. It all depended on various people hearing different sounds at different times. Conflict meeting desire? The analysis was not scientific, just haphazard and often the sounds would even sound like an angry man with lower tone levels. "WTF," was the term used by guests and workers alike.

Come for a visit—if you dare!

Chapter 1

HERE COMES JOHNNY

Johnny Ornelas was one of the lucky ones and smart too. He was a brilliant computer engineer and software designer. His privately-owned company, "Real Promises," grew big and fast, but Johnny being a strategist saw many others getting into the computer field, and realized that a bubble was building in the American economy based on easy credit, housing and construction companies borrowing millions, and the banks basing their viability on a floundering economy and not enough government regulation. Corruption and pyramid schemes ran rampant. Politicians were inept or out of touch with reality. The US Congress was at an all time low rating. Unemployment was high and people couldn't keep up with their mortgages and credit cards. Consumers loved the easy credit but many went bankrupt. By the time college kids graduated, they were $40-80,000 in debt.

The Washington bureaucrats just printed more money and told the citizenry that the economy was coming back to its former strength. It was a lie. The bureaucrats were lending millions and billions to people, entities, and nations that couldn't afford to pay it back; and the GNP was not keeping up with government spending. China bought up piles of the notes. It was better than any fire sale. The National Debt surpassed fifteen trillion dollars, and each citizen was responsible for about $134,000 of the debt.

Somewhere along the line, America decided to be "the policeman of the world," and was spending billions of dollars and sacrificing our soldiers on wars in Iraq, Afghanistan, Kosova, and Africa, and sending millions of dollars to the United Nations. America was delivering billions of dollars in foreign aid to countries that publicly hated democracy and voting, and denied basic freedoms and respect for women.

And then the financial bubble burst. Johnny wasn't a Bill Gates or a Steve Jobs in wealth or innovation, but through his analysis and cognoscenti, he knew that bad things were about to happen. He planned ahead and was spot on.

Johnny sold his company with only a couple of months to spare. He raked in fifty million dollars for a business that he had started in his father's garage for about five hundred dollars. His partners had dropped off or been bought out, so the final fee was all his. He wasn't a greedy man. He leaned more to generosity, and in his munificence, shared about $300,000 each to his remaining thirty employees. Several of the wives actually went to the company auditor, and thought maybe he had put in an extra zero by mistake.

Johnny had no wife or children. He had a few girlfriends now and then but no long-term special lady. Everything in his life was about computers, games and research. He thought he might become a game designer through another smaller company that he owned. But first he wanted to travel. Except for a few conventions, he had never been outside of San Jose, California, and his friends had told him about wonderful and exciting spots on the map. They also assured him that he would find suitable female companions along the stops.

He knew that many considered him a nerd, but his friends told him, "You might be a nerd but now you have millions of dollars. The ladies would want to share. You might consider getting rid of the black horn-rimmed glasses and the plastic folder that holds your pens and notes in the breast pocket." They assured him that he would do fine. But always detailed, he joined a gym, got contact lenses and a new hair style, and had a lady neighbor help him pick out some suitable clothes for travel and future dates.

For the next three months, he covered most of Europe and much of Asia. There was no problem finding a lady companion, but there was no one special. There were plenty to take care of his personal needs but as the weeks ticked away, he realized that he was looking for someone to settle down with and maybe build a family.

By a fluke, he landed on a Pacific island called Saipan on his way to Guam. His plane to Australia was diverted because of engine trouble lights. As he peered outside his airplane window, there it was—a beautiful blue-green gem of a Pacific paradise. He decided to layover for a few days. He soon learned that it was a USA island, and that it was a good location for tax breaks and operating a software game business. The weather and climate was just what he needed—an endless summer.

Johnny hooked up with a few locals—not the greedy politicians but with some sound, reliable Japanese and Filipino business people. They told him that it was near impossible to deal with the graft and corruption but one could usually get around it by knowing the ropes and what the laws were. They suggested that he just stay on course, be patient, and don't expect overnight results, and don't deal with the flimflam types that promised a three hundred percent return on the investment in just a few years. The Saipan economy was suffering just as was the rest of the world, except maybe China.

He spoke to several real estate agents, and through a Filipino contact, discovered The Californian Hotel for sale. The owners were elderly Chinese and ready to return to China for retirement and spend the sunset years with their extended families. Their children were grown and had developed properties on the US Mainland, and had no interest in returning to sleepy Saipan.

Johnny extended his flight again. Over a period of two weeks, a deal was struck with the hotel owners. The couple's children participated in the settlement via video conference and a translator. The couple was delighted to receive the full price for the hotel, even with the local economy in the tank and hotel occupancy rates bellying out at fifty percent.

Johnny found a large room near the front office that would become the center for his computer design business. He kept all the former hotel employees aboard and brought a bright young Japanese man, Yoshi Horoto on staff as his manager. Horoto was knowledgeable and efficient and his jocund personality made him perfect for the hospitality business.

The Chinese couple had managed the hotel themselves, but Johnny was the type of administrator to delegate to the best person available. He knew he was not yet ready to be a hotel manager, and besides he had games to design, and maybe take more trips to Manila or Shanghai.

He liked his new business card: John Ornelas, Proprietor—The Californian Hotel and the Barcelona Restaurant. He also liked being invited to dinner on Saturday night by his new Chinese lawyer, Jan Nan Wang. She was professional and a fine looking woman.

Now he had to meet with Oscar Martinez, his new accountant, about how to handle his income and reports to the IRS via Saipan-style. He had already ordered his custom designed computer system from the local Coconut Computer Services.

Johnny was putting in longer hours than ever before, and he loved it. There was still enough time to catch some Vitamin D rays at seaside.

Chapter 2

THE KNOW-ALL BELLCAPTAIN, BOBO CAMACHO

Bobo Camacho was the type of employee that knew everything, everybody, and could pinpoint where every little nook and cranny was located. He knew the water pipelines and the electrical outlets. Bobo had been with the hotel from the first day of opening, some twenty years before. He had gone from bellboy to bell captain, and all the activities and policies appeared to gravitate around him. With just a cursory observation, Johnny knew Horoto, the hotel manager, would have his hands full with Bobo, getting him under control and lessening his very strong and his informal supervision status.

"Ask Bobo" should have been on his nametag. Bobo was the man to see. His desk was strategically placed in the center of the lobby and he saw everything that went on and who came in. He was a problem-solver. For example, want a cake for a birthday? Want a girl for an hour or for the entire stay? Chinese or Korean? Where do I get a driver for an island tour? Can you find me a violin player for an evening romantic meal? My air conditioning unit is on the fritz—can you get it fixed? Where can I get some grass (marijuana okay but no hard drugs)?

The hospitality business is fueled by tips and lucrative assignments. As Johnny and Horoto would eventually discover—Bobo got a cut from every tip or referral. He wasn't greedy—ten percent would do. The employees had to pay a toll of five bucks for every extra shift they were able to work. The employees knew he was a money supply and also was the one to get them the extra shifts and favors. If the tips weren't forthcoming, then by magic, their shift hours would be cut. The personnel people knew about Bobo; he was like a weasel watching the rabbit hutch but they also knew he could arrange a discount on a new car and could make a phone call to get their beauty treatments at half-price.

Bobo knew many secrets. He understood what kind of women or male escorts the men preferred, and he knew the women who also liked women. The visiting older ladies could make a phone call to Bobo, and suddenly a handsome, brown "beach boy" would appear at their door to take care of their every need. The cougar ladies of the flower and hippy generations have found their true independence.

The politicians left themselves wide open for blackmail or for favors when he needed something for his clients. The politicos liked to visit the bawdy ladies in the back and hide their cars in a closed garage. One of the hotel guests was busted for drunken driving, and a few hours later after a phone call, a detective was dropping off the offender at the hotel. Most times, the criminal case never appeared on any court docket.

The previous owners let Bobo operate, and of course, he threw bits of money and favors their way. China is the land of bribes and "considerations," and they saw nothing unusual about Bobo's behavior. They should have known that Bobo was becoming a wealthy man, and was supporting both a wife and a mistress, a young lady barely out of her teens and a daughter of one his most important lady clients.

Horoto first noticed Bobo's involvement and possible collusion when he received a noise complaint from a guest who said it sounded like a sex orgy was happening in the next room. Bobo saw Horoto headed briskly to the elevator. He asked what the problem was. Horoto explained, and Bobo quickly volunteered to would take care of it. Bobo was red in the face and seemed nervous. The regular security man had gone home sick, so Horoto acquiesced. A few minutes later, he went to the "sex orgy" room to follow-up on the complaint and saw Bobo arguing with a half-dressed man. He picked up the last words of a conversation when the man said, "Okay, what's the deal? We paid you good money."

Both Bobo and the man saw Horoto approaching, and both realized they had to shut up before the problem got worse.

Horoto asked, "Everything under control?"

Bobo answered, "It's all good now. The man just got a little too enthusiastic about his girl friend."

A lady stuck her face through the crack of the door, and asked in a slurred voice, "Should we stick around or is it all over?" She wasn't wearing a stitch, not even a bikini bottom or panties.

The man said, "Just relax, honey. I'm coming back in, but you have to be quiet, okay?"

"Fine with me. You paid for all night. I grab a nap."

Bobo said to the man, "Sir, just go back inside. It's okay now, just keep the noise down."

"Swell then. Good night to you guys."

When the man went back inside, Horoto explained, "Bobo, you know the rules, only family and legitimate business people on this wing. If the guys want paid women, they have to use the back building."

Bobo flushed and brushed his hair back with this right hand, "There must have been a mix-up at the desk. I'll take care of it."

Horoto knocked on the door of the complainant, and explained that the problem had been taken care of, and made the hotel's apologies. Meanwhile, he saw Bobo on the cell phone, and heard the phone ring in the "sex orgy" room. Likely Bobo was taking care of business in his own way.

Later in the afternoon, Horoto was running headlong into island bureaucracy when he tried to get a building permit for a remodel in the restaurant kitchen. He was stalled at every turn by officials in public works, zoning, and natural resources. Bobo overheard the heated telephone call between Horoto and a government official.

After Horoto hung up, Bobo got the details and said he could ease the way for the building permit. Two days later, the permit was approved, and shady-lady Christy Cisneros had several new clients in the VIP suite. Horoto saw that Bobo could be a pain in the ass but also saw the advantages of having Bobo on his side.

A few days later, one of the cleaning ladies, Doris Fuentes, came in to complain to the personnel office about her hours being cut. She was frustrated and flummoxed. Just as Horoto was walking by, he heard the complaint and asked for details. Doris had no idea that she was ratting out Bobo. She assumed that was how everything worked at a hotel. She wasn't upset with Bobo, but was concerned with less money and not providing enough food for her family.

The personnel supervisor told the woman that her hours would be back to regular after a few days. Later, when Horoto asked, "Who cut the hours and why?" the supervisor said that she didn't know for sure but would look into it. Horoto didn't know that Bobo was arranging deep discounts on the supplies for the large wedding for the supervisor's daughter.

Horoto was no fool. He soon realized that large amounts of money for the hotel were being skimmed off the top by Bobo. He also realized that likely the entire staff was part of every type of scheme and discount. He saw right away Bobo often gave away the VIP rooms and even the marriage suite to his special friends. The pimp-man that supplied the ladies (*putas*) for the guests often used the suites for their own pleasures, in which Bobo occasionally joined in. This scam would soon come tragically to Horoto's attention—and the local police.

Chapter 3

FIRST VICTIM ON ORNELAS' WATCH

There had been several suspicious disappearances at the hotel long before Johnny ever took over; and two male residents had been found knifed to death in the parking lot.

After Johnny became the proprietor, the first strange circumstance soon surfaced when the telephone operator received a frantic phone call from Penthouse 4 right about brunch time. The female caller, in a thick accent, likely Russian, screamed, "Send the paramedics quick. My friend won't wake up!"

In the corner booth of the restaurant, Horoto and Johnny were having breakfast and determining how they might handle the situation with Bobo. They both knew that his removal would cause an uproar, and he would likely implicate other employees in his scams. The employees might just hush up, knowing that any admission could land them in trouble, lose their jobs, or even have to answer to law enforcement authorities.

After getting the information from the telephone operator, Johnny said, "Goodbye breakfast. We have to get up to the VIP suites pronto." He and Horoto headed for the penthouse suites.

While they were hurrying to the penthouse, Horoto alerted the hotel doctor by cell phone, Dr. Len Schwartz, who was on contract to provide medical services. He was discreet and often patched up people at the hotel, both staff and guests, and taken care of the "tourista" stomach aches. He had once treated a bullet wound and hadn't bothered notifying the police. Treating STD's was routine for him. He even carried a supply of condoms and ointments. He wasn't brilliant but was reliable and kept his mouth shut, which was all-important in the hospitality business.

Dr. Schwartz said his ETA would be about fifteen minutes. He was just finishing up the removal of a large hook from a fisherman's arm.

When Johnny and Horoto entered the penthouse, the caller pulled them into the right bedroom where they found a near-naked blonde girl, wearing only purple panties, sprawled across the king-size bed. Johnny checked for a pulse. There was none; her skin was bluish and her body had cooled way below the normal human temperature. CPR wasn't an option.

Johnny asserted, "Save your breath. She's long gone."

Johnny noticed a pile of various drugs on the nightstand, including several syringes. It looks like a potpourri of illegal drugs. He looked at the girl's arms and noticed that there was dried blood on a hole in her left arm. There was a burnt spoon on the bedroom headboard and a rubber tourniquet. She had regurgitated and the fluid was yellowish, laced with red blood. Johnny thought 'overdose,' just as Horoto said the same thing out loud.

Dr. Schwartz arrived and checked out the girl. He stated, "She's definitely dead. Likely an overdose. Looks like she was shooting up something, probably heroin. There have been some reports that the dealers are importing a new supply. Her supply might not have been cut—that's what killed her. The powder was too pure."

Horoto saw the female caller, now identified as Olga Sergenov, getting dressed and picking up her personal belongings. He said, "You can't go anywhere. You have to talk to the police." He paused and added, "We're the hotel management, and we want to know how you got here. There's no Russians registered at the front desk."

Olga mummed up and reluctantly sat on the sofa and put her belongings on a chair next to where she was sitting. She didn't appear drunk or doped up. She conveniently forgot to speak even the most rudimentary English.

The paramedics arrived and confirmed the naked girl was dead. The larger paramedic said, "We'll back off and leave the crime scene for the detectives. I suggest you not touch anything until the cops give the OK. They'll also call the medical examiner for transport—likely be an autopsy on this one."

Horoto said, "Thanks gentlemen for your help. Grab a cup of coffee and a snack in the restaurant on your way out. Just tell the waiter I said okay."

"Thanks, mon. Wish we could have done more."

A young patrol officer and two detectives arrived and took over the scene. They photographed the body and surroundings, and did the typical homicide processing and bagged up the drugs and syringes. They told Horoto and Johnny to stay and record their statements. He gave them each a pencil and paper, and told them to start writing. He tried talking to Olga, but the woman just shrugged her shoulders. Her vocabulary was probably limited to, "How much?" and "Where should we go?"

The older detective, Lt. Felix Cabrera, said to Johnny, "I knew you guys were running a whorehouse, but I didn't know about the drugs. Bobo must have been blind-sided on this one."

Johnny asked, "What are you talking about? Whorehouse and drugs—what are you saying?"

The detective replied, "We'll talk about it later. We've got to finish up before the body starts stinking." He laughed and added, "Now, that wouldn't be good for the hotel business, would it?"

The detective walked away, as Johnny said to Horoto, "This whole thing with Bobo might be worse that we imagined."

Johnny and Horoto completed their written statements—there wasn't much to say. The detectives called a Russian translator to talk with Olga. She wasn't cooperative until the detectives told her that she could either talk at the hotel, or they would haul her butt down to the jailhouse as a material witness.

Knowing what happens in Russian prisons and not aware of "due process" in the American system, she decided to talk. She said that she wasn't a drug user but Katrina had been developing a major problem. She liked everything from alcohol to meth, or whatever she could find, sometimes combining. She admitted that they were both prostitutes, and it seemed to bother Olga who had been to the university and wanted a professional career. Katrina said in the past that she was just happy to make a living and be able to send money back to her poor family in Moscow." She added, "I'm also one of the lucky ones in this business—I like sex and variety."

The young patrol officer wiped his brow, and swallowed back his saliva. There was soon sweat stains under his arms.

Felix said, "All that's good to know but we're trying to figure out what happened to Katrina. Who set everything up and who brought the dope? Who were you with?"

She answered, "Some guy in the hotel got us the rooms and the clients. I didn't know the men with us, but they seemed nice enough. They treated us okay. We each got a hundred dollars and all the dope and drink that we wanted. Some local guy showed up with more drugs; they called him Ricardo, and said he had some contact with the Yakuza, the Japanese Mafia. I've seen him around the hotels quite a bit."

Felix asked," What happened next?"

"We played around, and had some fun and laughs, and plenty of sex. We switched partners several times. That's what the men wanted."

"And?"

"We relaxed, and Katrina and the men did some more drugs. I just had a cold beer. The men had to leave at daybreak. They said they had jobs and had to get back home and ready for work."

"And what happened with Katrina?"

"I think she found some hard drugs in the pile on the dresser. I smelled something burning, a little stronger than a cigarette odor. The last thing I heard from Katrina was something like, 'Awww.' I slept in one bedroom and she was in the other. I knew we had to be out by twelve noon, so when I went to wake her about ten o'clock, she didn't respond, or even move."

"Did you touch anything?"

"No, nothing. I saw she wasn't breathing and called the front desk right away. You know everything after that."

Johnny asked, "Can I ask her a few questions?"

"Sure, go ahead."

"Who's the hotel guy that set this up?"

I heard the men talking, and one said, "These gals are great. We should give Bobo extra cash for these beauties."

"What do you know about Bobo?"

She answered, "I don't know him but I hear his name a lot. Apparently he's some big shot at this hotel, and he can arrange anything for a price."

"Have you been here before?"

"Four or five times. Mostly we get one of the penthouses. The hotel always sends up good food and drinks through room service. It's a good gig for a working girl. The tubs and bidets are fantastic."

Horoto looked at Johnny, and declared, "So much for any hotel profit. He's been skimming off the hotel for a long time, maybe his whole twenty years."

The medical examiners arrived and bagged Katrina for the morgue. The detectives allowed the translator, Horoto and Johnny to leave but asked Katrina to stay.

Horoto naively asked, "Wonder what they wanted Olga for? She already gave her statements. Her English is very limited."

Johnny rolled his eyes, "Who knows but that patrol officer was drooling all over his uniform."

"At least she enjoys sex . . . and multiple partners."

Johnny chuckled, "In her advantage, all part of the police protection and service!"

"Damn, I hope they pay her a few bucks for the families back in Russia."

Chapter 4

THE COMMISSIONER

After hearing all the stories and gossip about what had happened at the hotel, Horoto and Johnny met with the Police Commissioner to clarify the facts. They gave him a four-day notice for the appointment so that he might research the records and outline the cases and possibly the outcomes. They had been warned about the Commissioner, a do-nothing political appointee. He was handsome, made a good public relations appearance, but was dumber than a box of rocks. He hadn't had any police training and therefore, his troops had absolutely no respect for him. His nickname, which Johnny soon learned, was "Numb Nuts," which was right on target. He loved wearing his police uniform with badges and pins, which made him look like a supercilious Mexican general. He hadn't even written a parking citation, let alone made an arrest. The officers agreed to everything he said—they needed their jobs on an island with a thirty percent unemployment rate and you could be gone from the Department with the stroke of a pen or a phone call. Several government workers had been terminated from a short message on the FAX machine. Sadly as a consequence, the majority of the local cops were slow, arrogant and clueless.

The meeting was set for nine o'clock and of course, running true to his pisspoor reputation, the Commissioner showed up an hour late. He said that he been busy with several politicians on the hill, likely having donuts and coffee. Johnny watched the man carefully and saw that he was the very definition of hubris, self-centered and prideful.

He thought, "Who would hire this nincompoop? He couldn't make dogcatcher on the Mainland."

The Commissioner hadn't done his research but promised that he would . . . soon. He said that the department was in the process of updating their records, which translated to they were in process, or lost, or never written. The latter was likely because if there was no report, no case and no court filing—good way to assist influential associates. Johnny didn't like the man and tried not to let his feelings known.

Johnny asked if one of the investigators could join the group and maybe shed some general focus on the overall situation. He made a few phone calls and found an aged detective, Jorge, who made TV's Colombo and Monk look like geniuses. He had a vague memory that two guys had been killed in the parking lot but couldn't recall if anything was ever done. He had also heard that *brujas* (witches) had been seen floating through the corridors of several hotels but that had never been substantiated. At least, one had never been photographed or apprehended. There was also a rape and murder of a Japanese jogger on the nearby ocean trail and that three or four hotel guests had disappeared over the years. Those guests were Chinese who were on island to start businesses and were likely carrying cash. No suspects had been named.

The Commissioner and Jorge knew nothing of a Russian jogger that was missing or was kidnapped in front of the Duty Free Shop.

Jorge wasn't much more help than the Commissioner. They later determined through the community that Jorge had "retired in place" about ten years before. The police kept him around because he was from a well-connected family, and he made great coffee. He also fetched the donuts fresh out of the hot grease and obtained them at a "very reasonable" price.

They learned that the police had never solved upwards of thirty other homicides. The community wasn't overly concerned—most of the victims were nationals from other countries; but the unsolved murders had piqued his interest. Johnny wondered if there were noticeable patterns in the deaths, anything that could help with finding the killers.

Horoto and Johnny were frustrated. Both men were sharp and educated, and not accustomed to being stonewalled at every turn.

Horoto was particularly perplexed—his culture and upbringing made organization and competence necessary traits in life. During dinner, one of their vacationing Guam guests suggested that they needed to hire a professional private investigator and get all the past crimes clarified and organized, and possibly determine a pattern. Maybe the cases could even be solved and the culprits brought to the court in their orange overalls.

Johnny asked around the other hotels' management teams for a PI reference. One name kept popping to the surface—a local fellow named Carlos Montano, a Chamorro warrior with no sense of fear, either physically or of the politicians and island family networks. He was part owner of a local hotel, *The Beach Hotel*, on the water, but he preferred doing investigative work and leaving the hotel's management to his partner, Tom Parker. The partner was retired from the Los Angeles County Sheriff's Department and often assisted Carlos on his dangerous jobs.

Horoto also discovered that Carlos had an excellent reputation with the Chinese, Korean and Chinese communities; and the Filipinos thought he "walked on water." He was fair and straightforward. He was also from a "high," respected family.

Horoto invited Carlos to The Californian for an early supper. Carlos was right on time. Horoto noted that Carlos had handsome features, like a warrior featured in a Paul Gauguin south-seas painting, and that he was heavily muscled and gave off an air of confidence.

After Horoto had explained the situation and possible evaluation to Carlos, Johnny finished up his administrative chores and joined the conversation. They discussed Bobo and his involvement, and also island-wide issues. Within an hour, the trio were yakking and talking like old friends.

Carlos said, "Don't put the Japanese jogger on your mystery list—that's being handled by the FBI. The suspect was a little deviant from Palau. He's been identified and is now looking at a life sentence in the federal penitentiary for murder and hate crimes. It turned out that his family had been enslaved by the Japanese in World War II on Palau, and the anger that had been passed on from his mother and grandfather had been festering inside him. The young woman that was murdered had nothing to do with Palau, and had in fact been involved with solving societal problems as a Japanese social worker. She was one of those unlucky people who are in the wrong place at the wrong time. They won't be able to inject the little criminal with the drug cocktail. Unfortunately, there's no death penalty on Saipan."

Johnny noticed a dark brown dog sitting in the shade at the front of the restaurant. The dog barely moved and slightly wagged its tail when someone walked nearby. Carlos saw Johnny looking at the dog.

Carlos pointed at the dog, "That mutt you see is a pedigree Doberman Pinscher, aka a Dobie, and my canine sidekick. He goes with me everywhere and on several occasions, has saved my butt. His hearing is a dozen times better than ours, plus he has no fear with the heart of a wolf."

"Will he be okay with hotel guests? He looks like he's all muscle— about one hundred pounds."

"Nothing to worry about. Kids can pet him like a toy doll. He loves children, and grown people as long as they don't pose a threat to me, or someone under my protection. He's loyal and intelligent."

Horoto asked, "What's his name? Japanese tourists are always fascinated with animals."

"His official pedigree name is Zeus, the Greek King of the Gods. His nickname is "Big Red," and answers to both names." The dog opened his big lazy eyes when he heard his name. He slightly moved his back legs.

Carlos smiled, "Zeus is ever hopeful that some morsel might have fallen from the table, or maybe I needed some protection. He enjoys action almost as much as chow."

Carlos then said, "This has been an inchoate investigation but that's going to change. Firstly, let me tell you that I like your requests and ideas, and that Tom Parker will be with us the whole time. We've often talked about how any crime affects every one of our operations, and of course, threatens our family's welfare. It's gotten so bad that you don't let your kids out at night . . . and this is supposed to be a sleepy, safe island. The vitriol and inaction of the legislators make our jobs tougher, not only as crime busters but as parents every day."

Horoto asked, "Where do we start?"

"Secondly, just list every rumor or piece of gossip that you hear or can find. Keep me low profile on the property for a few days. I want to find out all about Bobo through my confidential informants. The word that I'm involved will get out fast via the island coconut express." He added, "I heard about the guys killed in the parking lot. It's not necessarily a mystery or a "who-done-it." The word is that it was a drug deal gone badly. Dumb-ass criminals. The two guys were known dopers, and they supposedly tried to cheat a Chinese guy from a Shanghai tong."

Johnny was surprised and said, "Now, that's just plain stupid. Don't they watch any Jackie Chan movies? Even Jackie has trouble with those guys."

Carlos laughed and said, "Also, I always say never mess with a billion plus people."

They worked out a fee acceptable to both sides. Carlos stated, "Don't worry about paying Tom—he just likes to get involved now and then. He says it makes his blood flow smoother and faster. He gets energized like the walking bunny."

As Carlos was leaving, Zeus slowly stood up and trotted along behind him. He glanced back at Johnny and Horoto, probably making a mental picture to go along with the smell. His shiny coat looked the shade of "mahogany" in the bright sun.

Horoto said, "Did you see the arms on Carlos. They're bigger than my legs."

"Glad he and Zeus are on our side!"

Chapter 5

AUDIT—MONEY GONE

Next day Johnny assigned Oscar Martinez to closely audit the hotel books for the past two years. Some of the items easy to crosscheck would be food service and liquor bills for penthouse rooms that weren't "officially" in use. Maid and laundry charges for rooms supposedly not in service would be another easy one. Oscar was sworn to secrecy and Johnny let him know precisely that word if leaked out, his head would be the chopping block. Oscar was apparently not on Bobo's informal payroll.

Johnny next called his new lawyer, Jan Nan Wang, and set up a romantic-style dinner in his computer room. He wanted to meet her in private, not necessarily just for romantic reasons, but to avoid letting the staff know that he was conferring with his attorney. He was assured that his head waiter could be trusted and wasn't beholden to Bobo.

The meeting with Jan Nan went extremely well. She personally knew Carlos' wife, Daisy, and their two children. She was pleased that Johnny had decided to get Carlos on the job and be able to clear up some of the mystery and intrigue about the hotel. Jan Nan said that all hotels have their share of myths and gossip but The Californian seemed to have had more than normal. She also knew that Bobo was involved in dozens of nefarious activities. His reputation was known far and wide and everyone had speculated as to why he wasn't fired or arrested. She knew that the previous Chinese owners had let him operate for their share of the under-the-table take, but through other Chinese, she knew the elderly couple was being cheated. She learned that the couple's children were glad that they had sold the business. She added that there was always a concern that the old couple would be robbed or just disappear like some of the guests. Like many Chinese not trusting banks, they were known to hoard cash.

She continued. "I suppose you know that the Chinese often only do a "cash and carry" business—no records. That is the way of China, with everyone trying to avoid taxes and government scrutiny watching your every move."

The relaxed conversation carried on for several hours. Johnny was optimistic that their relationship would go beyond business and law. After their eyes locked, Johnny decided to get more personal. He had already researched her status with his Asian friends.

"What about you personally? Are your married?"

"Yes, but my husband is in China. I went away to study law, and haven't seen him for ten years. We have a child together, a fourteen-year-old girl. She sends me news and photos on the internet."

"She must be a beauty, like her mama."

Without any hesitation, she took out her cell phone and logged onto the family photos. The girl was beautiful—he could see the family resemblance.

As she was ready to leave, she and Johnny made a list of things to be completed. Jan Nan would check all the hotel licenses, personnel policies, and any pending lawsuits or liability issues. The best Jan Nan could determine, there were no restrictions or discrepancies issued by the government. Possibly Bobo made sure that the hotel was in good stead with the governing bodies.

They hugged as she departed, and Johnny gave her a soft kiss on each cheek. Johnny saw it as a good sign when she didn't flinch or try to move away.

During the new few weeks, crime continued as normal during the economic downturn, but not at the hotel. Two Japanese golfers has their purses stolen from the golf cart on the ninth hole; a Russian tourist was robbed at knifepoint at one of the tourist attractions; two newlyweds' rental car was burglarized on Wing Beach while the couple was celebrating on the beach with their new intimacy; and a Chinese man was strong-armed but managed to escape and call the police. The assailants were described as local islanders, maybe Hawaiian or Chamorro.

Johnny said, "Horoto, do you see a pattern here? It's pretty obvious."

"Sure, the victims are off-islanders, not known around here. So the criminals are usually local because they can be anonymous with the foreign workers and tourists—outsiders wouldn't recognize them, but locals would." He added, "Two months ago, we had a Japanese diver raped and almost murdered by a local tour guide. He left her near-unconscious after a beating and naked on the reef as the tide was coming in—he figured she would drown and that would be the end of the investigation. She would be written off as a drowning accident."

With alarm, Johnny asked, "Did she survive?"

Fortunately, she came to and was able to wave at a fishing boat as it was coming into the harbor from a day of fishing. She was a great source of conversation in the bars after the rescue. After being twelve hours at sea in the hot tropical sun, the fishing guys thought they were hallucinating when saw the naked woman yelling and waving at them frantically from the reef. By this time, the water was starting to dangerously rise over the reef."

"They get the rapist?"

"The fishermen got her to the hospital and she was able to recount the day, and describe where she had hired the guide and rented the boat for diving. That jerk was in the jailhouse by next day, I think the police had no choice but to move on this one—the young woman was the Japanese Consul's niece."

But things were soon to change for the hotel. Johnny's mother told him often, "Beware when things are going too good—it will change and not for the better." When Johnny got the bad news, he had to smile about the old family admonition.

Chapter 6

MISS NORTHERN MARIANAS

Just like the Mainland, annual beauty pageants are big events on the islands and now the little girls that had been wearing princess dresses at Halloween were now in the big-time as they approached adulthood and trying to make names for themselves . . . and their parents. As usual in every contest, there would be a swimsuit and evening dress competition, a runoff, talent contests, and interviews, and eventually a young woman would be named Queen and she would have a court of four princesses.

It was pretty much rigged as to the nationality of the Queen and princesses. Each contestant had to sell a number of tickets to the pageant, and the one who sold the most got to be in the contest. Thus, like the elections, whomever had the largest family usually got into the finals. Daughters of foreign contract workers would hardly have a chance—the parents were making minimum wage and earning just enough to buy a bag of rice and a tray of chicken wings, and pay the rent. There wasn't enough money left over to buy a book of ten dollar tickets for the beauty contest.

Unbeknownst to Johnny, the beauty finalists had been placed in one of the penthouses. The five girls weren't the problem—there were plenty of beds for the guests. But the girls got to celebrating and soon the young men were attracted to the honey and the prospects of laying a beauty contestant. Of course, the lads brought along the booze and some grass, and soon the party was on. Still, that wasn't a major problem—it happens all over the world.

The situation escalated when the party went from happy to drunk in a matter of hours, and soon the lads were fighting to determine who got to bag the beauty queen or the princesses. By this time, the ladies had no choice, and they felt cornered up and ready to leave. Security was called, but the two uniformed men were outnumbered and backed off. The lads had pulled the telephones from the wall.

In most cases, Bobo would have been notified of the noise and would likely have got things under control. But even though he set up the penthouse for a favor to a pair of influential parents, he was over at his mistress' house trying to calm her down. She said that Bobo's wife had confronted her in the grocery market and had "disrespected" her in public. Bobo had his hands full with two feuding ladies. These situations usually ended up in serious headaches—Bobo should have known. Maybe the brain in his cranium wasn't doing his thinking.

With no other avenue, security followed hotel protocol and called Horoto. Johnny happened to be walking by the lobby when Horoto left his office. Horoto took him by the arm and said, "We've got some problems in the penthouse. The beauty contestant girls want to leave but a group of local boys won't let them go."

"How did they get there?" And then asked, "Have the police been called?"

"Not yet. I thought we'd see if we could handle it without a lot of bullshit and avoid the front page of the local rag."

"Sounds good to me. Let's go. Think we'll need stun guns or pepper spray?"

Horoto chuckled and said, "Hope not, but I might have to use my Tai Kwando."

"Some of those Chamorro boys are as big as Samoans."

Horoto said, "If they give us trouble, we'll just tell them we know Carlos. They should settle them down."

"Unless they're into drunken stupid!"

"There's that for sure."

As Johnny and Hoorto approached the penthouse door, they heard loud music and could hear intermittent screaming and shouting inside.

Two of the screams seemed to be coming from females. Knocking did no good, so Horoto used his passkey to get inside.

The scene in the room was something from a cheap drive-in movie. It was too surreal and mixed-up to be real. Two girls wearing just panties were backed into a corner by what appeared to be five drooling, nasty school boys. Pack mentality had taken over. The other three girls had apparently been able to maneuver themselves into a locked bathroom, and boys were banging on the door. Johnny was relieved to see that half the boys were not participating in the weirdness.

In his best low Japanese Samurai voice, Horoto shouted, "That's enough. Stop it right now!"

About ten athletic types turned and glared at the four hotel men— Johnny, a former nerd, Horoto, a small Asian guy, and two shaky security officers, wishing they had gone to work at the hardware store loading cement onto trucks, instead of facing jazzed-up, horny local guys.

Trying to imitate a strong command voice, Johnny said, "I'm the manager. Stop it right now and let the girls go!"

Half the group seemed to listen—the other half were probably too drunk, or into a mating frenzy that they moved towards Johnny, fists clenched. The group was noisy, clamorous, and set for violence. One of the guys yelled, "Let's kick their butts!"

Johnny asserted as he took out his cell phone, "I didn't want to have do this but I'm going to call the police and then Carlos Montano."

The crazed bunch stopped, and mumbled among themselves. The guys that hadn't been part of the assaultive group said, "Let's get out here before the cops come."

One of the mouthy dudes said, "Let 'em come. I'm not afraid of the cops. My brother's one of the officers."

Another said, "That won't help you if Carlos shows up. I saw that giant beat up four people at a wild party."

They started to move out. Johnny threw a couple of blankets to the girls so they could cover up.

Horoto said, "We'll be contacting your parents if there are any damages. Looks like that bathroom door is almost busted through."

After a few tough-guy profanities, the guys finally walked out. Three of them flipped off Horoto and Johnny.

The security men let out loud sighs. Getting beat-up for minimum wage didn't any sense.

Once the girls got dressed and settled down, Johnny said, "There's several ways we can handle this. It's up to you ladies. Did any of you get sexually assaulted?"

The girls nodded their heads "no." If you want to press charges, I'll call the police and you can make your reports . . . or you can notify your parents and have the parents work it out. The other possibility is to forget the whole thing. You're all over eighteen and able to make your own decisions as adults. This is a good lesson for you in adulthood. If the reports are made, everyone at the party will be busted for underage drinking, and I see some grass in the ashtrays. There's a possibility that you girls might lose your titles. I believe beauty contestants are supposed to lead good moral lives, and not be partaking of alcohol and drugs, and be in hotel rooms with horny men."

The Beauty Queen said, "I want to forget the whole thing. It just got completely out of control. It no one's fault in particular. We just invited few friends to enjoy the penthouse, and then this happened. Too many people." She asked the other girls, "What about you girls?"

They all agreed with the Queen. They wanted the whole thing to go away. It wouldn't do to have the whole sordid story on the front page of the local rag.

Horoto said, "Okay then—here's the deal. You work it out with all the parents involved. I'm going to get together an estimate for the damages. I'll have it ready in a few days. I expect you to be straightforward and deal with the parents. After you get the estimate, I expect payment within a week. Understood?"

Johnny added, "Get all your stuff together, and we expect to hear from you soon."

Just as the group was leaving, there was a flurry of car alarms going off in the parking lot. They looked out the penthouse window, and saw three dark shadows smashing car windshields with sledge hammers. Then they saw the security guys chasing after the jerks.

Horoto asked the ladies, "Do you know those guys?"

Several answered, "It's too dark to see. Too far."

Johnny took twenty pictures of the penthouse and the damage and debris. Horoto locked up the penthouse and said, "The cleaning crew will have a big job tomorrow."

"And the parking lot maintenance crew also."

Horoto commented, "I thought this fiasco was going too smoothly."

Johnny added, "Means more calls and reports to Jan Nan. Good thing we have an attorney aboard."

Horoto smiled and quipped, "And plenty of work for Carlos. He'll get names."

Chapter 7

NEWS FROM CARLOS

News spreads fast on the islands. Next to the importance of sex and romance, gossip is real close, and that's mostly talking about "who's doing whom," or "did you hear so-and-so is single again?" So when Carlos showed up at the hotel for breakfast, it was no surprise that he had the names of the "windshield smashers" and who the troublemakers were at the party gone amok in the penthouse.

Carlos showed the names to Horoto and Johnny. He asserted, "Some of the boys are from prominent families. They obviously didn't learn any discipline or self-control in their homes."

Horoto and Johnny read the names and recognized several as the children of politicos and businessmen.

Horoto asked, "What's our next move? The police know about the vandalism in the parking lot—should we do a follow-up relating the overall situation to the penthouse problem?"

Carlos said, "I think we can put this whole situation behind us, and get restitution for all the damages. The girls are still against making a scandalous spectacle out of the whole mess. Since they're adults, they're worried that their names and photos will show up on TV. The Queen is particularly worried about losing her crown."

Johnny asked, "So, what do we do now?"

Carlos looked determined, "I've talked to several of the parents. Some of them are in my extended family. They want the whole thing to go away also, and are contacting other parents about footing the costs for the banged-up cars and the hotel damage."

Johnny said, "That's good. So the money for the damages will be forthcoming?"

"Yep, it's a done deal. I believe they will pay up." He continued, "Now we can move onto the two dead guys in your parking lot. That turned out as we thought. Two local guys—Tommy Lopez and Woori Rivera—were the jerks that decided to cheat the Chinese. Apparently they had done it several times, and they didn't heed the subtle messages from the Chinese suppliers. It was simple for the Chinese—send down a hit-man from Shanghai as a tourist. He did the deed and headed back to China the next day."

Johnny asked, "Weren't the Chinese concerned about getting two new local salesmen?"

"That's never a problem, here or on the Mainland. Always a few knuckleheads willing to take a chance for easy money, and their own personal supply of dope."

Johnny said. "Looks like the books are closed on this one. No great mystery here. You read about dope deals going sour everyday in the US . . . dead bodies dumped in the mountains and found floating in the lakes."

Carlos continued, "The case will never go to trial. There are no witnesses or evidence. All hearsay and rumors. Besides, even if the secret killer was identified, China wouldn't allow an extradition to Saipan."

Horoto asked, "Then how about the ghosts and tao-taomonas?"

"These sightings are always happening, like Sasquatch being spotted in the North California woods, or the double size Himalayan tiger being spotted in Tibet, or the Loch Ness monster in Scotland. I always enjoy hearing about the image of Jesus Christ being spotted on a tortilla in Mexico, or God presenting himself in a burning bush on the Mojave Desert. Sometimes too much drink might be involved or a person is looking for attention, maybe a religious zealot that wants to be the next reality star on television"

"So how about the ghost being spotted at the hotel?"

Regarding Saipan specifically, tao-taomonas are spotted every year, sometimes at a fiesta where there's plenty of beer or some weed in the shadows, or a swoosh of wind and a white plastic shopping bag blowing down the corridor of a hotel or a government building. Tom Parker and I have reports at our hotel also."

Horoto asked, "So you think it's all bogus?"

Johnny said, "I've already got reports of sea monsters on our beach, but according to other beachcombers, the "big thing" might have been a shark or killer whale searching for food, or a seal showing off."

"I'm out quite a bit around the island and have talked to dozens of people about the ghosts and monsters, and even about green space aliens from other galaxies. Nothing has panned out and I noticed that most of the sightings have been solo—no other people involved except the witness to those events . . . but do we really know for sure?" He shifted his eyebrows up and down a la Groucho Marx.

Johnny laughed and stated, "There could be more dimensions on our earth. But right now, there doesn't seem to be more investigation needed. I notice that these strange entities cause no threat or harm to anyone. People just get scared of the unknown and unexpected."

Horoto and Carlos agreed.

Carlos declared, "I sure would like to see one for myself. Now, moving on to the guest disappearances from the hotel. Some big questions here."

Johnny summarized, "You just need to drink tequila more often. Remember the old Mexican saying, 'One tequila, two tequila, three tequila, the floor!' But in our island sightings of monsters and hobgoblins, the more you drink, the more strange creatures come out to play!"

Chapter 8

THE MISSING GUESTS

Carlos volunteered the following information about the missing guests—a Chinese couple out touring and a Russian jogger on Beach Road near the Duty Free shops. The cases had never been completely solved, and when he asked the Police Department for reports, only the entry page of the report had been checked off. The front page of a long report had been filled out since Johnny and Horoto had visited the commissioner. There were no narrative and investigation notes. Both incidents were listed only as "missing persons" and no mention of theft or possible homicides, and in both cases, the victims had been carrying money—unknown amount. Both cases happened in daylight in December of last year.

Carlos retired from the Police Department, White Collar Crime Section, about a month after the incidents. He remembered both cases quite clearly, because there had been formal inquiries from the victims' home countries. The victims had never returned home after their island visits and the families were worried. When he heard about the modus operandi of stolen money and personal property, his first thoughts went to a habitual criminal known as Raffy Rodriquez. Raffy had committed numerous crimes involving violence and theft; but when he checked jail records, Raffy was incarcerated at the time for assault with a deadly weapon. He had hit a victim with a steel bar after the victim caught him in the house red-handed.

Carlos said, "It appears that the police did very little in solving this case. It always seems to drop in priority when the victim is from another country, and very little gets done, and even less information is recorded."

Horoto asked, "If the victim is from another country and we depend on tourism, wouldn't it make more sense that would be extra effort? Pull out all stops . . ."

Carlos stated, "There you go again, trying to apply logic. The best avenue would be, of course, crime prevention with regular patrols and placing security at the main tourist sites."

Frowning, Johnny asked, "Did they get a description of the clothing, jewelry or watches that the victims might of had on them? And how much money might be involved?"

"No, none of that was done. I already sent inquiries yesterday to their home countries—maybe the officials will check with the families for more details. As soon as I get some information, I'll check pawn shops and ask around to see if anyone recently came up with a windfall of extra cash."

Horoto said, "All the victims were staying at our hotel. When housekeeping checked their rooms, they were bare, like someone had come in and stripped away everything, including suitcases and clothes. They called the police about checking the room for fingerprints or any other clues."

"Then what happened?" Johnny asked.

"Management made the rooms available to the police for a week, double-checked with them and they said that they had no fingerprinting equipment, and the one guy that did fingerprinting, had quit and moved away. So the crew cleaned the room and put it back in service."

Johnny asked, "Has any of the other hotels had missing guests?"

Carlos laughed and said, "Not for real. We did have one lady notify us at our hotel that her husband was missing. We did some quick checking, and it turned out he was in jail for drunk driving. He was so far out of it, that he couldn't tell the jailor what hotel he was staying so the jail could make a notification. As soon as the man finished with his mug shot, he fell completely asleep, and didn't wake up until the next morning. In another case, there wasn't a happy conclusion for the wife. They were a fun-loving, passionate Aussie couple. For the husband, it was probably quite satisfying for what we jokingly call "a happy ending."

Horoto guffawed, "What happened?"

"He got back to our hotel okay, but he was freshly showered and smelled like the whorehouse he had just visited. The dummy still had the lady's "massage services" card in his wallet. He made some lame excuse for his absence, was shown the door by his wife, and ended up at the front counter asking for another room. I was walking by at the same time, and told the receptionist to give him a room on the opposite side of the hotel at a special discounted rate." Carlos paused and added, "I then asked him how things were going? Can you sort it out?"

He was smiling from ear-to-ear and answered, "Mighty fine, mate. Mighty fine, the finest kind. I didn't know your island ladies had read the Kuma Sutra."

"Did they leave together next morning?"

"Believe it or not, they made up at breakfast and left ricky-tick fast. I did hear her say, 'You owe me one.' The last we saw of them, they were heading for the transit bus for the airport, hand in hand. Hominids are damn interesting to watch."

Johnny said, "Yeah, they are. It's unfortunate that our cases won't have a Hollywood happy ending. It's just not right that people go on vacation and get whacked by some hoodlum."

Carlos asserted, "Well, maybe we can get them some justice."

Horoto added, "I know we will." There was that Samurai voice again!

Chapter 9

RAFAEL "RAFFY" RODRIQUEZ

Carlos paid a visit to see Raffy at the jailhouse. Raffy was doing ten years for a series of robberies, burglaries and assaults. In California, he would be part of the "Three Strikes, and You're Out" program, meaning he would be doing a life sentence for the felonies. But on the island, ten years was a long sentence and likely to be shortened for a parole. The island was too short of budget revenues to keep feeding the criminals for a long time. The funds were needed for more important priorities like the politicians' travel, VIP meals and entertainment, and fancy rental cars. On the same day a month before, a criminal was released from custody and committed another crime, while the story next to it in the local newspaper showed the governor and his entourage eating five-pound lobsters in Los Angeles. It was another one of WTF situations.

Raffy had not let himself go while in prison. He looked strong and confident, and maybe matured since Carlos saw him some three years ago. He heard that Raffy was even attending the GED program, and as hard as it was to believe, Raffy had been spotted at the Catholic Mass.

Carlos met with him in a private room off of the guards' office. The officer told him if he needed help that there was a buzzer under the table top. Carlos said, "Thanks but I think I can handle Raffy."

The guard said, "Maybe before, but that fool has been lifting weights. After watching him for a year, I do believe he is trying to turn his life around . . . or getting more prepared for his next robbery."

Carlos and Raffy shook hands. Raffy said, "It's been awhile. Heard you're out of the cops and running a hotel."

"Yep, all true. My place is called "The Beach Hotel, right on the water. Tell your friends to stay away from my guests."

Raffy smiled and said, "Look, man, I'm twenty-five years old. I wanna get out this joint and start living my life. I'm sure missing the ladies."

"I need some information about several of the guests at The Californian Hotel who are missing, probably dead. A Chinese couple and a Russian jogger near the Duty Free building. We already know about the Japanese jogger case. What's going on with the jail scuttlebutt about the crimes? I know it wasn't you—you were in the jailhouse at the time."

"Maybe I planned and had my boys do the jobs."

Carlos looked at him straight in the eyes, and said, "I don't think so. You never worked in a gang before, and your never intended to kill someone. You always left your witnesses to testify."

Raffy smiled and said, "That's why my cellmates call me stupid, for leaving the witnesses and victims to testify."

"Must have been your good Christian upbringing. Listen now, I need your help on this one—I have no trail to follow and the cops did a slipshod investigation on both cases."

Raffy asked, "Now for the one thousand dollar question . . . what's in it for me?

"You know the ropes. Pro quo quid, you scratch my back, I scratch yours. You help me and I'll do everything to help you with your parole. You even get out a coupla years earlier."

"And then what. Who will hire an ex-con and my parole won't allow me to leave the islands? The parole officer will be holding my passport."

"If you're straight with me, and keep up your GED and prep for the future, I'll hire you at our hotel. You know Tom Parker, my partner. He's a good guy and has taken a chance on three ex-cons, and it's working well."

"What job would I do?"

"You'll start at the bottom like everyone else, laundry, deliveries, cleaning, and gopher work. Then you move to the desk or beach duties. You're not a sexual offender, so I can have you interact with my guests, guiding, checking out boards, working in the beach snack bar. Much is up to you—how hard you work and what your aptitude and attitude are like."

He chuckled and said, "Then I can't be the assistant manager right away?"

"Not a chance. I know you're anxious to see the ladies, but if you mess up there, you're out of a job. Zero tolerance for drugs also."

Raffy asked, "Then, how can I help you? I'll tell you what I know, and I'll keep my eyes and ears open in the jail."

"That's good but don't get yourself killed as a snitch, and also beware of the guards. Watch out for accidentally slipping in the shower. Many of the guards, cops, and bad guys are related."

"What should I tell them when they know I'm talking to you?"

"Tell 'em that I'm working on old crimes for an insurance company. And don't worry about the microphones and cameras in our little room. Those have been disabled for years. Just make a mental note of what you hear or see, and anything about the guards repairing the old recording equipment. There are very few secrets in a jailhouse."

Carlos didn't hear from Raffy for two weeks. Carlos was wondering if he had changed his mind about cooperating and sorting out the jailhouse chatter.

Meanwhile information and photos of two watches, three gold rings, and two sets of earrings were emailed back from China concerning the missing Chinese couple's property. The couple had also been carrying about fifteen thousand in US dollars that they were going to send by Western Union to relatives in New York. The New York relatives indicated that the money had never arrived. Or maybe the money was to buy drugs.

Carlos had one of the ex-cons, Jesus Gonzales, working at his hotel to take the photos around to the pawn shops to see if anyone had pawned the watches and jewelry. The disappearances were over a year old, but with the high price of gold it was likely that if the pawn shop had taken in the items, that they might still be sitting unsold in the shop's safes. There just wasn't a lot of extra money on Saipan to buy gold necklaces and earrings.

Raffy called Carlos and set up a meeting in the afternoon. Raffy asked him to bring in some real "freedom" food from outside the jail. Carlos called his Korean chef at the Beach Hotel and arranged for a special meal for Raffy and threw in some Kim chi and eggrolls for the guards.

Raffy and Carlos talked while Raffy devoured the food like a long lost dog getting his first meal after days lost in the wilderness. When he finished he let out a loud burp and said, "That was good. Love the strong garlic. There's even enough for a meal later."

Carlos smiled and said, "Glad you enjoyed it. Now then, why am I here? I generally don't make meal deliveries to jailhouses." Both men looked through the glass and watched the guards chugging down their food. They had already checked to see if there were functional recording devices in the room. There were no signs of new construction on the walls or floor, and nothing in the room that could contain cameras or tape recorder, like a baseball hat, small boxes or books.

Carlos said, "Give me the news. You know I'm anxious to see if Bobo is involved in any of this."

He answered, "It appears that Bobo has his fingers in just about everything, including the money till at the hotel. But he's just a petty thief and a manipulator. He would steal if he had the chance, or shag your sister, but there's no indication that Bobo has been doing the big stuff like murders and robberies. He does a little drug business but only home-grown marijuana. His brother has a farm high on Mount Topachau, does coffee and a special strain of grass loaded with THC. If anything, Bobo knows that his schemes are dependent on tourists also."

"How about the disappearances?"

"I'll tell you right up front, the FBI identified the right guy, Gregorio Santos, for kidnapping and probably killing the Japanese jogger. The word is that guy was a deviant and a real asshole. No one ever knew when he would go off. He had been in a dozen bar fights, and hurt several guys with a knife. He has convicted sex crimes on his rap sheet. No one ever called the cops because they had arrest warrants from the court or were "people of interest" in other crimes."

"Oh yes, the underworld. I remember it well. Dirty business with late hours."

"Yeah, but you're back in it."

"Just helping some friends. Besides all these miscreants hurt our tourist industry. You'll see this when you start working at the hotel. Many of the guests are scared about going outside the hotel grounds." He asked, "So Gregorio is still among the missing—the FBI never nailed him."

"That seems to be the case. He could be hiding, or got to Guam on a boat and skipped the immigration checkpoint."

He paused and asked, "How about the missing Chinese tourists? And the Russian jogger?"

"Not much word in the jailhouse. It's slow because I don't want them to get suspicious about all my questions."

"Learn anything?"

"Some of the boys were talking about the Chinese couple. It was a good hit with plenty of money. The guys killed the man right away, and then raped the girl before she died. Then they buried them out in the jungle near Marpi Point."

Carlos asked, "Any names?"

"The guys that did it apparently are not in jail right now. Some how, the Yakuza is involved somewhere. The names are really being hushed up—no bragging going on. Everything I've got is second or third hand. But there is one guy involved called 'Ricardo.' He came over from Guam and is a relative of one of the killers."

"Nothing on the Russian jogger lady—any little piece of info?"

"No, nothing on that case. Maybe it was just one of those where a lone wolf made a move at the opportune time and there are no others involved. If he doesn't go around boasting and banging his chest, we might never know."

"Yeah, it's usually the bragging that bring those jerks down . . . or a disgruntled girl friend who is seeking revenge." Carlos added, "Just keep listening. Every little piece of info helps."

"Will do. Make sure you bring some more tasty Korean food on the next trip."

Carlos dropped by the Police Department to see all his old buddies. Once they were talking, Carlos ran the name "Ricardo" through the Saipan and Guam computer banks. Four names came up and all four were habitual offenders: Ricardo Ramirez, Ricardo Lopez, Ricardo Wabol and Ricardo Iglesias. Carlos didn't know any of the subjects, but they were definitely starting points. Judging by their criminal records, he figured they would be easy to find—he knew the type and their habits.

Chapter 10

JAN NAN WITH THE TEAM

Johnny made another date for dinner with Jan Nan to get updated on the crimes and hotel status. He knew there was more to the date but at least, he had a legitimate reason to meet with his attorney. Gossip had told him Jan Nan was definitely not involved with her husband in China, and that she had had a few affairs over the years, but was now unattached. In China with her husband, she had a 14-year-old daughter, Su Lee, who she loved dearly.

Johnny smiled to himself, and could feel the excitement building inside. He felt like a teenager going out with the girl of his dreams. "Change thoughts," he thought. He managed to get himself calmed down by reviewing the hotel books and considering several new policies about financial accountability.

Dinner was set up in the same private office. Jan Nan was on time, and more radiant than ever in her form-fitting basic black dress. He saw that she was wearing her "gold," and that disturbed him thinking about her going home in the dark. But he figured he could lock up her gold in the hotel safe, or he could have security officer escort her home.

But neither possibility was necessary. No one had ever explained the three-date rule to Jan Nan, or maybe it didn't exist in China. This was only their second time together privately.

Jan Nan discussed the licenses and restrictions on the hotel, and even had a copy of the Natural Resources Impact certificate which allowed his hotel guests to frolic in the ocean and for him to operate boats, water skis, and allow his guests to fish in the lagoon. Everything was in order.

She said, "I know Bobo is causing a lot of trouble and ripping the hotel off, but on the other hand, he keeps everything going along smoothly—no hassle. Much of what he does is right in harmony with the Asian way of doing things. Everybody gets a piece of the action, so he's on board with the hotel prospering. Hotel full—he makes more money also. He apparently treats everyone fairly, just at your expense. Bobo is totally in support of the hotel—his wife and mistress depend on it."

"So how I do handle this guy, especially legally?"

She laughed and said, "Again, the Asian way. Call him in and issue some strong warnings about his skimming, or you can call it theft. Threaten to call the police—he knows he has been wrong. You have to be strict and make him accountable. I wouldn't suggest you fire him but keep his skimming to a bare minimum, and order him not to intimidate the other employees."

"How about him running the girls?"

"Reality check! Every hotel has some of that action going on; and its been going on forever, way back to Egyptian and Roman times. The Chinese emperors always had a pack of concubines for their personal services and for his special guests. The secret is to keep it out of sight, and restricted to a certain area, like your back wing.

"But absolutely no dope. I'd even have him drop the marijuana sales. If the boys want dope or betel nut, let them go get their own. Lot of sellers in nearby Garapan. Be clear that there's no supplying from the hotel."

Johnny changed the subject and asked, "How's your meal? The steak has a special marinate, a recipe handed down from my late-great grandmother. She was a fantastic cook. If she were still alive, I'd have her training the hotel chefs."

As she was dumping on the Tabasco sauce, "The steak is really good, and I like the fresh vegetables."

"That's the other secret. All those vegetables are fresh, grown right here on our island."

They finished up and moved out onto the balcony to watch the zillions of stars. It was a new moon, and the stars were particularly bright. Johnny had brought along two glasses of Bailey's Crème on ice.

Johnny reached over, took her hand and gave her soft kiss on the lips. Again, she didn't flinch. He said, "You are a beautiful woman."

She softly spoke, "Thank you, Boss. I was wondering when you would get around to seeing me as a female, not just a lawyer?"

"The noticing part started on Day One but I've had to keep our relationship professional. I don't want my own lawyer suing me for sexual harassment."

She then moved her chair closer and kissed him deep and hard. She asked, "If I sexually harass you, will you fire me and then sue me with another attorney for a breach of ethics?" She chuckled and added, "I've heard about you computer nerdy types. All you think about is hard drives and floppy disks."

"No floppy disks here. I say we sexually harass each other. I'm about to burst on overload."

She took the pad and beach towel off the lounge and neatly placed them on the floor. She said, "This seems like a nice spot to co-mingle our files."

He exclaimed, "Perfect!"

She joyfully said, as they lay down on the mat, "In front of the Creator and the entire universe."

He said, "I like your red panties."

"Red is the lucky color for the Chinese."

Jokingly he said, "I hope Bobo isn't selling tickets to the show."

"Who the hell is Bobo?"

After a few hours of sweet love, Johnny fell into a deep, dreamless sleep. Jan Nan was already out and curled up under his right arm and was completely motionless.

Chapter 11

SECURITY OFFICER AT THE DOOR

Just after the morning re-acquaintance of intimacy, they were jolted awake by a loud knock at the door. Johnny slid out of bed, patting Jan Nan on the bottom.

It was Alfredo at the door out of breath, barely gasping, "I think we've got another disappearance."

"Okay Al, calm down and relax, and tell me what happened." Al was fat and heavy, and was borderline diabetic. With a wide sombrero and a longer mustache, he would look like the original bandito from the movies.

After a few deep breaths, huffing and puffing, he related, "We went to pick up the luggage and do the room checkout on Penthouse 4. No one answered the door and when we went inside, everything had been tossed and thrown around. The couch and upholstered chair had been sliced with a knife—the cotton padding was everywhere. The registered couple, Bob and Betty Thompson, was not in their room, and the bed was still made. The telephone was missing and two lamps broken."

"With all that breakage and noise, no one called the front desk?"

"No calls and there were occupants on both sides of the room We checked with them, and they're okay, no injuries or complaints."

Johnny dressed quickly. He asked, "Have you told Horoto? Did you check to see if their rental car is on the lot?"

"Horoto is off with Carlos on some early morning fishing expedition. He's on the way back—we got him on his cell phone. The desk is checking on the rental car. Alfredo's cell phone rang. He then said, "Appears that the rental car is gone—a red Toyota Echo, plate # YZT394."

Johnny called the Police Commissioner. He hadn't arrived at work and the dispatcher didn't know when he was coming in. Johnny then spoke to the Watch Commander who promised to send over a uniformed crew and maybe a detective. Johnny was hoping it wasn't the old man, Jorge, but then again, he might bring a box of fresh tasty donuts.

The uniformed crew arrived in just a few minutes. They appeared to be fine young officers—close haircuts and clean, pressed uniforms. Johnny figured they were fresh from their Academy graduation.

The older officer, Juan, took down the initial information. Johnny asked if they had a camera to record the crime scene. Neither did. So Johnny took a hundred photos of the scene, and said he would email them to the officers. They couldn't fingerprint the tables and lamps because they didn't have any equipment or dusting powder. They actually weren't trained in evidence recovery but they had seen a good movie on TV as to what to do.

Horoto and Carlos arrived. Carlos shook hands with the young officers; he had worked with both their fathers. Carlos said to Johnny in private, "Those are good guys. I'll bet their fathers are hoping they don't get screwed over and end up with the 'I don't give a damn' mentality."

The police department had not taught the young officers how to put a police "special alert" on the radio regarding the missing couple. So Carlos taught the officers the procedures and made sure the radio broadcast, besides the local agencies, also got to the Guam officers and the federal agents. Alfredo called the airport—the Thompsons nor anyone else had used their tickets. The couple had not been seen since the previous night in the hotel dining room. Their passports were still in the hotel safe.

Jorge's detective son, Felix, arrived thirty minutes later. He smelled of stale cigarettes, and onion and garlic. The Department had not found the Thompsons, nor had their car been recovered.

Horoto asked the detective, "Where does one hide a red Echo on this tiny island? It should be easy to spot."

The detective replied, "Sometimes the crooks drive the car into a garage, and strip it piece by piece for parts. Other times, they just drive it off a bluff into the ocean. The boat patrol is checking the shorelines around the island now."

There was a knock on the door. Alfredo said, "The newspaper reporters are here, as well as the TV crew. Should I let them in?"

Johnny answered, "Okay with me. Felix, what say you?"

Felix asserted, "No, keep 'em out. They'll just get in the way."

Johnny thought to himself. "What better way to get the news out fast, and have the whole community looking for the Thompsons?"

Carlos was apparently thinking the same way, and said, "I'll talk to them outside."

Felix shouted, "What are you trying to do, Old Man? Jockeying to take over the case? You're retired—one of the old-timers."

Johnny noticed that Carlos jaw locked tight, but he controlled himself and declared, "Just calm down. I'm trying to help and I'm on retainer for the hotel. I work here."

Felix slightly lowered his eyes and said, "Okay. Just don't get in my way, or I'll report you to the Commissioner and Governor."

Carlos shrugged his shoulders and as he leaving to meet the press outside, he said, "Ouch! My career is in jeopardy." As he opened the door to leave, he added, "Do what you got to do. Just don't threaten me or I'll mention that to the press also."

Felix turned and walked away.

Horoto said to Johnny, "See what the good cops have to contend with?"

"BS, my friend. Let's go hear Carlos talk to the media."

The press conference went well. Carlos had obviously taken classes in handling the press, likely at a FBI training. He relayed the info professionally, and said there would be recent photos of the Thompsons when he received copies from the family over the internet. Meanwhile he had copies of the photos in the passports which he distributed."

"How would you describe the missing couple?"

"Both Caucasian Americans. Both tall—both thirtyish. The man is about six-foot even, brown and brown. The woman is about five-foot, nine inches, blonde and blue."

When asked what the Thompsons were doing on Saipan, his only answer could be "Tourists, I suppose." He didn't know for sure

The reporters asked to speak to the lead detective. Felix sent one of the new officers to the press conference with a curt replay, "No comment. Call the Commissioner for a statement."

Over the next week, the trail went cold. Even television addicts of detective shows know that the first 48 hours is vital in investigating missing persons and homicide cases. It appeared that Felix and the Commissioner never watched the shows, or had never experienced professional police training. There were no media statements from the Commissioner. The Governor issued one statement through his lackey PR man, "We have nothing to report. The solution to this matter will be forthcoming when substantial information is developed." No one knew what that meant.

Weekend hikers found the Echo deep in a forested ravine. They called the cops, and the responding officers had the vehicle towed back to an outside storage yard. They didn't check around for fresh graves or other evidence that might lead them to the culprits. But the hikers had made a cursory check, but they hadn't found anything noteworthy.

The windows had been broken out in the crash down the ravine. The officers didn't process the car right away for evidence. They said that would be done in a few days—meanwhile, the car was exposed to several rains and blistering heat. A dozen people also had access to the sedan. Any recovered evidence would be questionable and legally useless.

But that didn't matter—the detectives never got around to properly processing the car. One detective went out to examine the car, and he noted that the keys were still in the ignition and that were red stains on the floorboard. There was no personal property in the car, and the bumper jack had been removed.

Carlos checked the airline itineraries to see if any "Ricardos" had visited Saipan from Guam before or after the disappearance of the couple. There he was, one day before two days after—Ricardo Lopez. Carlos called one of his FBI pals, and checked Ricardo Lopez through every criminal computer system in the USA and Canada. He also checked out Bob and Betty Thompson. He was curious about what their Saipan visit was about.

Carlos obtained Ricardo's booking photo and his prints. He had a rap sheet about a yard long, mostly petty theft, some marijuana drug sales and interestingly enough, he had been busted for a homicide but had been released on insufficient evidence.

Bob and Betty were no angels either. They had dabbled in fraud, bad checks and were suspected of running drugs from Canada to the USA, and vice-versa; the reports indicated that the couple took amphetamines to Canada and marijuana from Canada to the USA. The truckers had a saying about 'never run empty on the turn-around," because you have to buy fuel both ways. It seemed that the Thompsons were practical and thrifty.

If they had figured on branching out into the Pacific, their plans didn't go well and went askew when they ran into the likes of Ricardo, and possibly the quiet, almost invisible, Yakuza.

Carlos asked that he be sent the rap sheets and photos of the Thompsons.

Chapter 12

BODIES FOUND

Hank Flores, the father of one of sharp cops, called The Californian Hotel to ask to speak to Carlos. The hotel telephone operator told him that Carlos was at The Beach Hotel. Hank called Carlos and got himself invited to breakfast.

When Hank arrived, Tom Parker had just sauntered in with his wife Cocina, hand-in-hand. They all sat down together.

Cocina took a plate of hot cinnamon rolls and passed them to the men. She said, "Enjoy. The fresh coffee is in the colorful decanter, right from Manila."

There was general agreement of *masarap*, good and tasty.

Tom said, "Hank, you can talk freely in front of Cocina. She can keep a secret." He paused and added with a smile, "Well mostly."

Cocina laughed, "If it's about work, I never talk. But if it's about love affairs, I have no control over rumors and *tsismis* (gossip). There's no controlling of a Filipina's tongue when wagging over so-called secret news."

Hank chuckled, "No problemo. It's all about work . . . possibly the missing Thompson couple."

Carlos asked, "What's up? Got something definite on the Thompsons?"

"Not sure. Two bodies have been dug up by stray dogs. The bones are human but with little info in the burial site. The bodies were naked and there were no personal belongings and clothes, and no knives or guns. No tattoos or distinctive features."

Tom asked, "Identified yet?"

"No, the detectives are going through their old files—might be bodies from an old case or maybe a new one. They don't think it's the Thompsons. All the flesh is gone and it appears the bones were in the ground a long time. It was a macabre scene—especially while we were digging up bones under flood lights. We had to get the bones before the night critters moved in and took what was left."

Carlos said, "Could be our missing Chinese couple. Timing is about right."

Hank said, "The Medical Examiner arrived and bagged up the bones. He'll have one of the doctors do an autopsy, and retrieve any tissue or bone marrow for DNA. But we all know the problem there: no DNA on file and no family to work out an identification file."

Carlos asked, "How about the dental? Do the x-rays?"

"Yep, got x-rays and photos. We only have six dentists on island—so I have a young officer taking the x-rays to their offices for a possible match. But if it's the Chinese couple, they were here just a few days before they disappeared. Not likely there will be a match-up with a dentist."

They finished breakfast, talked about the weather and fishing, and the lack of tourists. The hotels were optimistic that Homeland Security was going to allow Russian and Chinese visitors into Saipan without a long list of bureaucracy and rigmarole . . . and expensive documents. When he was leaving, Hank said, "Thanks for breakfast. Please tell Chef Guangman the cinnamon rolls were beyond words. I'll keep you posted if I hear anything."

As it developed, the bones belonged to a female and a male, both adults. With burial in the ground, the flesh usually decomposes quickly, especially in the wet climate of Saipan, and rats and a myriad of insects and lizards take care of the rest. Wild cats and dogs do their share also. Nature's recycling at her best.

Investigation with China authorities and family indicated that the family would provide DNA samples if required. The police indicated that if it was the missing couple, Liu and Nae Wang, the two had been on and off in the drug trade. There was a pending case against Liu Wang, and if he had returned to China, it was likely he would be imprisoned and even facing the death penalty for selling drugs. The China police supervisor said through a translator, "Better this way. We can save a bullet."

A family member said that the couple should have about $15,000 in their possession, which they had borrowed from their relatives for 'an American investment," and to send to relatives in New York.

When Carlos mentioned the money to the Chinese supervisor, he had another quick, short retort, "Dopers always screw over each other. Liu must have been thinking about bringing drugs back to China for a big profit. We've closed off the border at the Golden Triangle of Burma and Thailand for drug smuggling. Hard to get opium and cocaine through there now. Get caught with drugs, the execution will probably take place the next day."

Carlos said, "It appears that Liu was trying a different plan—Saipan route."

Gruffly, the Chinese supervisor said, "Money and drugs never mix well. It seems the young woman also paid the price. Bad friends, bad luck." He added BFD. Obviously he had been watching American movies.

"Seems that way. Aloha and mahalo."

Chapter 13

DISCO NIGHTS AND
THE PORNO QUEEN

Horoto knew about the sexy woman living on the fourth floor of the east wing. No one really knew how she earned her money, but she always paid her rent and utilities on time, and had the latest versions of cell phones and iPods. She had a brightly colored parrot tattooed on her right shoulder, a butterfly on the other shoulder, and a "love me" tramp stamp above the crack of her butt, impressively showing when she wore her skimpy bikini. Yoga had done wonders for her flexibility and gracefulness. She was totally into health and exercise—no smoking and no drugs. She did enjoy Sangria wine, which was delivered every month. The delivery man was often pushy and obnoxious, and twice she had to call security to ask the man to leave. She wouldn't accept money from the delivery man—her payment schedule required more than strictly business. She had to like the client.

Horoto figured it wasn't his place or judgment concerning her life style. She had many gentlemen callers but there never seemed to be any trouble or fights . . . or loud parties. He was worried that she might become a statistic on the missing person/homicide lists because she often left late at night for her assignations with gentlemen acquaintances and occasionally with beautiful older women.

Her name was Lucy and she was a 10+ in the rating category. No doubt she was a bi-sexual nymphomaniac. She got along with everyone at the hotel, including other women and staff members, and was fondly called "the porno queen." She didn't earn her reputation by selling tickets to beauty contests and charity events, and was affectionately remembered by her callers for her many kindnesses and expertise. Seldom in life did so many men (and women) refer to a lady as "the best piece of ass on the planet."

Lucy liked luminaries when she was making love—nice scented candles putting a golden glow on the room. She provided condoms for the men and sex toys for the lady clients. Unlike most women in her profession, she would kiss and take it slow. She never rushed and treated the men like kings, which of course, helped them to finish faster and she was on to her next date.

Bobo was her main contact, and she had to be booked weeks ahead for a dinner date and evening cocktails in her apartment. Because of her monthly cycle, she took a week off every month just to relax and follow-up on her hobbies of arts and crafts. She could croquet a bedspread, make an aloha blouse or do a stained glass window. Often her clients took home a piece of artwork, besides a long-lasting memory.

The hotel had a disco that operated Friday and Saturday nights. The music started about ten o'clock and the DJ was a wild, crazy local guy called "Willie Boy." This was a man that worked at the Health Department all week as a laboratory technician, but on the weekends he let loose. He organized theme nights, one being "black clothes only," another "girls pay," another "plaid schoolgirl skirts," another "silly hats," and the biggest night of all was the "no panties" night. The latter night was a money-maker for the hotel—the dance hall was usually packed to the rafters. Horoto had to admit that he liked to go to the disco on that night, with girls dancing with their mini-skirts sans underwear. When the horndogs got speculating, he loved the expression about whether or not the girls "trimmed the hedges."

Needless to say, Lucy was one of the stars. She was so fit that she could dance the night away, and still have the energy to entertain her special guests. Booze at the disco stopped at two o'clock, but often the DJ and dancers kept going until daybreak. The disco noise and commotion didn't bother the other guests. The festivities were off in the back in a separate building and had thick, sound-proof walls.

On this typical, bright sunny, glorious day, a security officer knocked on the door of Horoto's office. It wasn't Alfredo this time, but the man, Alfonzo, who could have been his twin brother. Horoto thought that next time they did a new hotel brochure that he would feature the look-alike security officers.

Alfonzo related that Lucy hadn't been seen or any evidence of her being at the hotel in recent days. She didn't pick up her mail at the front desk or re-newed her monthly rent. Her sporty bright-yellow Mustang was still in the parking lot.

Horoto asked, "Has she done this before, just left without telling us?"

"No, it's unusual and that's why we're worried. She is usually in touch with the front desk."

"Okay Alfonzo, I want you to tell Johnny to meet me up at 'Porno's' room." He blushed sheepishly when he used her nickname. He added, "Call Carlos also. Then call the police for me. See if there have been any accidents, like she might be in the hospital or God forbid, her body might be on a slab in the morgue."

Another security officer followed Horoto with a passkey. Horoto knocked loudly on her hotel door several times and then entered. The apartment living room was neat with only a few of her art projects here and there on the tables. The bedroom door was closed.

Horoto knocked on the bedroom door several times, and when no one answered, he entered. Shockingly, there she was, the Porno Queen naked and spread-eagled with her arms and legs tied on the four corner posts. He knew it was her—he remembered her tattoos. She was definitely dead and the body was still well-preserved. The air-conditioning was going full blast. The coolness and the surreal feeling of the room reminded Horoto of visiting his dead mother at the Japanese funeral parlor. Except for Porno, she wasn't left with any sense of dignity and had been posed as a whore by her killer.

He called the front desk on his cell phone, and instructed the receptionist to call the police and the medical examiner. There was a dead body to investigate. He and the security officer touched nothing except the doorknobs when entering.

Johnny and Carlos arrived shortly thereafter. Carlos said it was definitely Lucy and that she had entertained him several times before he was married. Johnny asked, "Should we cover her up?"

Carlos said, "No, leave her just the way you found her." He took twenty photos for later confirmation of the crime scene before the cops messed it up. He noted some dried substances on her crotch area, on her breasts and on the sheet." He took close-up photos.

He said, "Likely semen. Will be good for DNA if we can collar the culprit to match it with."

The Commissioner and Lt. Felix Cabrera came bustling in, and asked where the body was. Horoto showed them the way and explained how he had found her.

Being his normal PR self, Felix said, "Now you guys clear out. We have work to do."

The Commissioner added, "You guys go back to your jobs. We'll take care of everything. We'll contact you if we need anything else."

Carlos said to Horoto, "There's more to this than us getting the 'bum's rush.' There's something foul afoot."

Horoto gave a Carlos a puzzled look, as much to say, "Huh?"

The security officer said, "Bobo told me that several of Lucy's clients were high in government. We all just assumed she might have been one of the governor's massage girls."

Johnny said, "It may be that the Commissioner is protecting or covering up for someone. I'm glad I got those photos, before they cleaned up the crime scene. I want you to tell housekeeping to save the sheets from that bed for evidence. If I were a betting man, I would say that those cops won't save it for lab analysis."

The Medical Examiner took possession of the body and personal belongings. Horoto made copies of her passport and recorded everything with a signed receipt, noting that he turned over $3028 to the examiner. He knew that Lucy had a young daughter back in the Philippines, and he intended to make every effort to get Lucy's property back to her family.

Johnny asked the Medical Examiner, "What happens to the body?"

"If no one claims the deceased, we'll bury the body in the pauper's cemetery near Lau-Lau Beach. We keep the remains in the refrigerator at the hospital for thirty days, and if no claimant steps forward, off to the burial site."

They watched as a gurney rolled in to pick up the body, and Lucy was unceremoniously loaded onto to the bed of an old rusty pickup truck which was serving as the official government hearse. Terrible ending for anyone, and especially for Lucy who counted on dozens of people to love and support her. She had made many people happy. Most of these people could never step forward; they were part of the dark side of Lucy's complicated life and style.

Carlos peered out the lobby window and saw Bobo sitting in the shadows, smoking a cigarette. His head was bowed, his shoulders slumped. Was it just business or something else?

None of the hotel staff were interviewed by the police, which included Horoto and the security officer who found the body. Incompetence followed by incompetence, and was Bobo somehow involved?

Johnny asked to no one specifically, "Ever feel discompubiated—out of touch with reality?" Another WTF moment.

Chapter 14

JOE AND JOY APPLEBEE

Horoto walked into Johnny's office just as Johnny was finishing his call. Johnny was smiling like crazy and jumped to his feet. He said, "Horoto, you won't believe this—my friends Joe and Joy Applebee are coming to the island on vacation and to celebrate their tenth anniversary. They want to renew their vows."

"Sounds great. We can fix up the wedding chapel with new paint and lighting."

"Mahalo, my friend, but they want to get married on the beach at dawn—you know new day, new beginning, and all that romantic stuff."

"Just a matter walking down the stairs to the beach. Won't be a long drive and no worries about DWI."

"They're both cops from Sacramento. They're both on the straight and narrow, and drunk driving or disturbing the peace isn't in their thought patterns. They'll be here in a week."

Carlos joined them, along with Guangman carrying a plate of hot cinnamon rolls, and a large pot of strong Korean coffee. After picking out the rolls and coffee, Johnny let everyone know about the wedding plans. He asked Carlos to set up a judge or minister for the ceremony. He asked Guangman to prepare a special wedding buffet.

Guangman asked, "May I prepare some Korean food, as well as the American entrees?"

Johnny answered, "Oh yeah. These are adventuresome people. There are plenty of Asian restaurants around Sacramento."

He continued, "Ask your wife Seuhchill to find Joy one of those beautiful Korean long dresses. I know she will love it. They're about the same size."

Guangman answered, "Done . . . and now I must get back to our guests." He waved and headed for the kitchen.

"Probably on the way to dig out some of that aging Kim chi from one of his special caves," said Horoto.

Carlos said, "I tried some of that five-year recipe at the last meal. It was tasty and very memorable. My innards burned for about a week."

They all laughed and poured some more coffee.

Johnny asked, "Any developments on the Thompsons?"

Carlos asserted, "No, nothing. Zero, nada. The autopsy doctor concluded that the two found bodies were not the Thompsons, DNA indicated Asian genetics. And nothing on the teeth ID with the Chinese couple's bones and skull."

Horoto said, "Looks like we're stymied unless the wild boonie dogs do some digging."

Carlos exclaimed, "Okay, I know this is crazy and maybe completely nonsensical . . . but if the Applebees are adventuresome and trained cops, how about we use them as decoys? They can flash around wads of money and we can borrow some gold and diamonds to ignite the bad guys."

Johnny said, "It sounds tempting but they have two little kids back home with Joy's mother. They're trained professional officers, but I can't imagine those little children growing up without their mother and father."

"Want me to pitch the idea to them? You can't be blamed for something stupid that I do."

Horoto said, "Let's do the wedding and party, than we talk to them. They plan on staying three weeks. They'll have plenty on their minds now—why worry them now?"

Johnny said, "That's make perfect sense. Now, let's get planning. Carlos already lined up a minister for the ceremony, plus let's find a great reggae band. We'll stage the whole affair on the beach, including some dancing in the sand and some fantastic music. Will be like Frankie and Annette in California kicking up sand to a fast beat."

"I've got one of the penthouse suites reserved for them."

More typical glorious days passed on Saipan. The sun came up, went down; tides came in and went out. Sunsets busted every imaginable color in the spectrum. Johnny never tired of the salty whiff of fresh air at high tide. It was all part of the Creator's master plan. There was no news on the Thompsons and the Russian jogger's killer, Gregorio. He still hadn't been found and arrested.

The Chinese couple's DNA from the bones was analyzed with their family members and confirmed in 99% probability that it was Liu and Nae Wang. Because they were suspected drug dealers, the Chinese government wouldn't provide funds to transport the remains back home; and their family was close to poverty. Thus, it was decided to bury the bones in a plywood casket in the pauper's cemetery. Burial confirmation and photos were mailed to the family with condolences from the island of Saipan. None of their property or money was ever recovered.

Joe and Joy came in three days before the wedding to get acclimated. Joy commented, "Damn, it's hot and humid here."

Johnny came back with the typical response to Mainlanders, "Yep, it's the tropics, but you'll get used to it in several weeks. Just go to the beach and feel the trade winds in the afternoon. Much of the adjustment is mental. Sit under a swaying coconut tree and order a daiquiri or margarita. You'll feel comfortable in no time." Johnny thought to himself, "Maybe not. Some women never adjust and want to leave after a few days, or sit in air-conditioning for most of their vacation. The makeup runs and the hair goes all frizzy. But at least Joy was trying. She was up early for her morning jog and a quick dip in the lagoon."

The dawn of the wedding arrived, standing in the shallow surf bare-footed, the bride and groom were decked out in the finest flowery aloha clothing. He wore white pants—her skirt was white—and both wore *mwar-mawrs* and *leis*
. It was one of those perfect days for an outdoor wedding. The weather cooperated completely—not even an occasional shower. The minister and the other members of the wedding party all showed on time, and no one was yet drunk in the breaking of a new day. That might

come later with all the varieties of booze, mimosas and Bloody Mary's. Guangman had his work crew in place and the barbeque with breakfast entrees had started hours before.

Half way through the ceremony, Johnny noticed the women sniffling. Carlos' wife, Daisy, was dabbing her eyes, and Jan Nan was lightly crying, her hand tight on Johnny's arm. Tom Parker's wife, Cocina, clenched her eyes closed, trying not to be too obvious about her feelings. As the bride and bridegroom read their vows to one another, promising undying, eternal love, Johnny looked at the others in the audience. The women, mostly Asians, were all sniffling, including the wait staff and the older office accountants and receptionists. He noticed that several of the men had teary eyes. So much for the granite-face, no-emotion stereotype Asian. Apparently the so-called stoic Oriental was another groundless myth—they certainly enjoy weddings and are sentimental.

The wedding was undoubtedly touching, and especially in the bright dawning of a new day. It captured the heart and the emotions of love. After breakfast, the plan was to swim and relax. The "old" newlyweds might just wander off and enjoy the comforts of their private room. Preparation for the afternoon reception was well underway with the reggae music and hours of dancing. The bride was going to wear the traditional long Korean dress. Cocina and Seruchill planned to join her, all wearing different colored dresses from Seuchill's closet.

Breakfast was set up on twenty weather-beaten picnic tables and benches. After a dozen toasts to the happy couple from the audience, Seuchill whispered to Guangman that she had to go the grocery store and pick up a few items for the afternoon buffet. Carlos' wife, Daisy, volunteered to go with her. Zeus had been watching the wedding activities from the shadows but when he saw Daisy and Seuchill jumping into the hotel SUV, he quickly maneuvered his way onto the back seat and went to sleep almost immediately. Zeus was doing one his favorite things—sleeping in a moving vehicle with the wind blowing across his body, just like a big baby.

Daisy looked back and said, "Look at that dog—he can actually smile."

Chapter 15

BIG MISTAKE—BIG DOG

After finishing up their shopping, Daisy and Seuchill stopped at the new coffee shop, Java Joe's, for a latté made from the recently arrived aromatic roasted coffee from Columbia. Their conversation switched from the delicious coffee taste and the wedding plans for Joe and Joy, to wondering what was happening at the Californian Hotel. They figured it might have been a central starting point for island drug deals, or maybe it was just a coincidence. They were sorry about what happened to Lucy, the Porno Queen; they liked her as a person. They didn't approve of her life style but through a Western Union friend, they knew she was sending hundreds of dollars to her family in China. It was hard to decipher if her death was related to the disappearances. It was a continuing mystery.

While splitting a nutmeg scone, the ladies looked out the window and saw two chopper motorcycles stop in a cloud of dust and gravel just in front of the shop's entry steps. The two riders palavered for a few minutes and then walked up the steps. Their beat-up leather jackets said "Death Squad" on the back.

The two noisy, large local galoots walked into the shop. They noticed Daisy and Seuchill sitting near the front window. The men were both drunk and tired after a long night of drinking and carousing, and had moved into the obnoxious and loud stage. One of the men with a two teardrop tattoo under his right eye, lumbered over to the women and said, "What do we have here?"

He turned to his T-shirt friend and declared, "These Asian bitches are always horny. They are born to reproduce—they love the boom-boom." Tattoo man reached over and touched Daisy's breasts.

Daisy slapped his hand and firmly said, "Go away, or I'll call the police."

Tattoo man said, "Good English and good lookin'—this will be more fun than I thought." Daisy started to grab her phone inside her purse. He shouted, "Touch your phone and I'll kick your ass."

Meanwhile sensing major trouble, the coffee attendant reached for the wall phone to call 911. Tattoo Man quickly moved to the phone, pulled his fixed-blade knife, and cut the cord. T-shirt Man just stood in awe; like he was some kind of outlaw trainee or likely he had a room-temperature IQ on a cold day.

Daisy reckoned, "Here's our chance. She grabbed Seuchill by the arm and the women ran to the front door. Tattoo Man ran after them and was about to reach them but Seuchill dropped a chair in front of him. He stumbled and cussed. They made it to the SUV. It hadn't rained so the windows were down. Once inside, they locked the doors electronically, and as Daisy was rolling up her window, Tattoo Man reached through the window and made a swipe at Daisy with his knife. She dropped to her right side, and managed to roll up the window. Tattoo Man's arm got caught between the window door frame and the pinching window. T-shirt ran in front of the SUV as though he was going to stop the vehicle if it accelerated.

The dummies didn't know that a huge surprise was waiting inside. The windows were tinted; they couldn't see into the back seat area. Zeus had awakened and grabbed the intrusive arm, half hand and half wrist. Instinctively he decided to hold onto Tattoo Man's arm with his massive teeth. He knew something was wrong—the man was screaming and was threatening Daisy. Now, the outlaw guy didn't know what to do. He yelled for Daisy "to roll down the window and get the damn dog off his arm." He dropped his knife inside the SUV.

His voice had no effect on Zeus. During defense training, he only listened to Carlos and Daisy, and other close family members and friends. Tattoo-Man was not part of this known group so he decided to hold on. Blood was dripping down the inside of the door, along with pints of dog drool. Seuchill had called the police on her cell phone. Daisy later said she had heard bone crunching but didn't want to call off Zeus until the police arrived.

Ten minutes passed—more blood and begging from Tattoo Man. From a warped sense of loyalty, T-shirt Man had decided to stay in front of the SUV to stop the women. When he heard the police sirens, he switched from "Fight to Flight' in nanoseconds; but by the time he cranked up his bike, the police were on him.

In this case, the police were professional and helpful. The officers got the two jerks under control and tied a tourniquet on Tattoo Man to stop the bleeding. They took the report, actually writing and filling out forms, and waited for the Medics to show up to take care of Tattoo Man's arm.

The officers summarized that Tattoo Man's arms would need extensive repair but could possibly be saved. There is no rabies on Saipan which worked in Tattoo Man's favor. One of the officers fantasized what Zeus would have done if either of the ladies had been injured.

Daisy said, "I know what would happen. That dog loves his family and would fight to the death if he had to. He'd go through window glass and take out the offender."

The officer said, "Yeah, I know about Dobies. They were bred for protection and guard work, but they also make great family dogs."

Seuchill asked, "What have you heard about the disappearance of the Thompsons and the Russian lady?"

The older officer said, "Nothing new. Gregorio Santos is still on the lam. No developments."

Daisy asked, "How about Lucy, the Porno Queen?"

"That case is weird—actually off limits. There's only a few people in the Department in the 'know.' A very strange situation"

Daisy asked when the older officer was alone, "What do you think, totally on the QT?"

"I didn't say this, but she had many 'high power' guests—couple of them at the top levels of government."

"Do you think one of them killed her, had her killed?"

The other officer walked up, and the older officer said, "Okay ma'am. The report will be ready in a few days." He gave her the case number, and off they went with the two now-subdued tough motorcycle gang-bangers. Sobering up in many ways would make them humble.

Seuchill asked, "Did you get any worthwhile information?"

"Not much about Lucy; but it's as we thought. Some bigwigs are involved. I remember some of the gossip from the workers that two senators and a budget director had been spotted coming out of her apartment."

"Sometimes those fools have a lot to lose. I suppose they get desperate and stupid."

"Or egotistic and selfish." Daisy lamented, "We never got to finish our coffee."

"We'll try for another day, and keep our eyes open for drunken motorcycle riders." Seuchill added, "You are very brave. I've never seen you in action before."

Daisy smiled, "I'm fearless when I'm with my dog because my dog is fearless. He has the heart of a wolf."

Seuchill continued, "Zeus sure saved the day for us."

"Now, I hope our husbands don't go crazy about the assault. Carlos often gets impatient with the police. Hopefully the two officers will write a good report and the detectives will get off their backsides."

Seuchill was learning about the local cops, "The problem now will be with the detectives. Most cases they just throw away."

"Or the courts let them walk out on probation and a letter of apology to the victim."

Two tow trucks showed up to haul away the outlaws' motorcycles. As the motorcycles were loaded up, the operators were definitely not concerned about scratched paint and dented gas tanks. Very few people like outlaw bikers.

Chapter 16

UNDERCOVER CAPER

Carlos and Tom later learned from their police buddies that the two arrested outlaws were not involved in any of the hotel's cases. They sold some dope but mostly from their relatives' farms. One veteran officer said, "Even a dope dealer wouldn't hire those fools. They could screw up a B-movie about lazy cops."

Carlos guffawed, "Or finding a haystack in a pile of needles." He added, "It's too bad 'cause some of the guys and gals on the Department are pretty good, but the bosses don't want them to work making cases— mustn't increase the performance standard of none. And they might identify some of the perpetrators as relatives of high mucky-mucks in government or business. Whenever a detective got too close to a graft or corruption case, the Commissioner or the Attorney General would utter those well-known words to the troops, 'No more—your case is of low priority. Go do something else.' That meant of course, 'Don't do anything,' and translated to go along to get along, especially if you liked your police job.' Unfortunately the recent political hires and hostile environment had caused an obvious 'dumbing down' of the Department."

Days slipped by and still nothing about the Thompsons, the Russian lady's suspect, or Lucy's killer. The investigation about the two Chinese victims had stalled, even after finding the bodies.

Johnny and Carlos decided it was time to ask Joe and Joy to give them a hand on the cases. By this time, the couple had visited most of the beaches and saw the Polynesian shows, and was even thinking about leaving a few days early and exploring Hawaii before they headed home.

Johnny, Horoto and Carlos met with the couple over a gigantic lunch of barbeque, fresh fruits and the scrumptious cinnamon rolls. Johnny considered pitching the idea of them posing as decoys by visiting doper spots and letting everyone know that they had plenty of money and were trying to buy drugs to take home to California.

Joe and Joy were experienced cops and knew body language and the different choice of words and the intonation of voice. Before Johnny made the request, Joy asked, "Okay Muchachos, what's going on? You characters are not acting your normal selves."

Carlos spoke first, "You got us. We didn't know how you would act when you heard our request. We know you have kiddies back home and right now, you're on vacation to get away from the crime business and general BS."

Joe said, "Yeah, so what is it?"

Carlos said, "We've got no right to ask this, but we need your help." Carlos explained what they had in mind, even to the point of Joe carrying a large roll of cash that they could flash around, making sure the word got out that they were loaded with beaucoup bucks.

Knowing that many couples make decisions without saying a word, Joe and Joy looked at each and slightly raised their eyebrows; and within a few seconds, Joe said, "We'll do it. We like to catch bad guys plus if we could come up with something that would help to get the mystery and negative stench off the reputation of the hotel, then it's worth it."

Joy added, "Seems to be a 'Hail Mary' approach but it's all we have right now. I don't have much sympathy for dope dealers, but I would like to solve the cases with the murder of Lucy and the disappearance of the Russian lady, likely also a homicide case."

Joe asked, "Okay, how do we start? Also, you have to remember we didn't bring any fire power with us. We weren't expecting any action with felons."

Carlos said, "We have .40 calibers that I can come up with."

Joy said, "That'll work for me. That's what I carry back home, and Joe can handle any gun."

Carlos explained all the hot spots where all the dope and sex deals took place, also illegal gambling. Carlos thought it would be productive to flash the roll at the gambling spots, and then meander around the general area until a dope seller came up. He said, "We'll have you wired the whole time, so we'll hear the conversations between you and the criminal types. You might have to watch for an opportunistic robber all the time—he might get to you before the dope sellers. Young thugs are known to lurk in the dark alleyways."

Joy responded, "Be good to take down an armed robber. Be harder than hell to explain to the bosses back home."

Johnny said, "It's risky all the way around. Undercover work always is. We don't want you to get hurt or get into any kind of trouble with your jobs."

Joe said, "We'll try it. It's our choice and we want to help out. That's what we do. It's corny to say but we really believe in making our communities safer. Cops put their lives on the line every day, so none of this is new to us."

Joy reached over and patted Joe on his hand—another example of a couple in harmony.

Johnny's heart was pounding. Never in a zillion years could he imagine he would be involved in an undercover deal. He was out of his computer element, and it felt damn good! He felt like shouting "shazoom" and changing into a super-hero costume.

Joe and Joy went out on the caper several times. They even booked into the nearby Fiesta Hotel where they weren't known or had been guests before. The trail was cold, and the response even cooler. They might have been spotted at the Beach or Californian hotels, or been eyeballed with Carlos . . . or maybe there was a spy in their camp. Johnny thought about Bobo and his network.

Joy even went shopping by herself, and no one hit on her, for anything. On the last day, Joy said, "Damn, not even a guy propositioned me for a drink or romance, and I was wearing a near-see-through skirt and blouse."

Cocina said, "Now that stinks. Not even a pick-up line from a tourist or a drunken jerk. That's not good for a woman's ego."

Seuchill added, "You both must be really known. The word is out—the bad guys probably have photos of you on their cameras and internet."

For whatever reason of no contact, the couple's time for departure came up and they were to fly out next morning.

To recognize Joe and Joy for their extra work, Carlos and Tom organized the finest of the going-away luaus, right on the beach. There were ukuleles and dancing hula girls, and bamboo torches.

With total appetite, Zeus filled up on hand-outs and large rib bones . . . and he remained bumptiously friendly. Carlos could sense that something was bothering his furry sidekick—maybe a few strangers at the party he didn't recognize. His ears turned down several times while he was sniffing about.

After the meal, Joe said to Joy, "Our last night and a full moon. Shall we take a very private walk?"

"Oh yeah, my handsome hombre. You are my hunko man!"

"Yippee iyoh ki yay! Hunko man, eh? You best be careful, my fair maiden."

She laughed and answered, "Raging bulls don't scare me."

Before they were hundred yards down the beach, and before Joe's hands had a chance to wander to the nether regions, a voice from the dark, "Hey Gringos, wanna buy some dope?"

The voice came from within the dark jungle. They were lit up by the full moon and silvery sea while walking at the waterline.

Coincidence or a set-up, were they sighted in to be the next disappearing couple? Frustration in self defense—they had already returned their pistols to Carlos.

They also sensed they were being followed by something in the jungle bushes.

Chapter 17

DOBIE ON THE JOB

"Yeah, man. We want drugs," shouted Joe. "Come on out."

He whispered to Joy, "When he breaks from the dark, run like hell and get Carlos. Tell him to bring a pistol. I'll try and handle whatever this guy has to offer."

She hesitated, "I can't leave you, you know that."

"We don't have time to argue. You run faster than me. Go like hell." A shadowy figure started from the dark onto the sand lighted by the moon. "There he is, go now!"

Joy ran back like blazes to Carlos and Johnny. Thank goodness, she heard no gunshots. A brown fast-moving giant dog almost knocked her over running towards Joe.

The shadowy figure from the jungle approached Joe but before he got close enough to use a knife or club, Zeus was on him. Zeus had seen something in the man's hands which he perceived to be a threat. Zeus leaped into the air and took the man full blast on the chest. The man fell backwards with Zeus definitely aiming to clasp his throat between his mashing teeth. Sand was flying in all directions.

Joe saw that the man was carrying a brown bag and not a weapon. He used his command voice, and said, "Zeus, it's okay. Let him be."

Zeus stopped his attack on the man's throat and merely placed his paws on the man's chest to stop his movement. Joe ordered, "Don't move He won't hurt you unless you try to get up. My wife has gone to get Carlos, the owner." Joe noticed slight bite impressions on the man's neck—but no skin broken.

Joe called Carlos on his cell phone and gave a 10-4, everything was under control. Within a few minutes, Carlos and Joy, accompanied by Tom and Cocina were at his side. Joe noticed that Cocina was carrying a four-foot club, the sturdy ones made from mangrove wood. Tom was huffing and puffing, trying to catch his breath.

Carlos walked over to Zeus. Carlos patted him on the head, and said, "Good boy." What was left of his bobbed tail was wagging like crazy. If dogs could grin, that's where Zeus' expressions were centered. He was proud that he had done the job for his master.

The man under Zeus yelled out, "Get this damn dog off of me."

Carlos chuckled and said, "Don't you be insulting my dog. You're in no position to be making disparaging remarks about a helpless canine."

"This mutt is not helpless!"

"There you go again, calling my pedigree Dobie a mutt. If you keep this up, I'm going to let Zeus have you for breakfast."

"Okay man. Please get your beautiful dog get off of me."

Joy said to Joe "Aren't you glad we gave Zeus snacks from the table. Zeus remembered and he obviously decided to be your friend."

"He probably thought I was carrying more snacks."

She said, "More than that. He really bonded with you." Zeus was simultaneously watching Carlos, Joe and his "captured prey."

On Carlos' command, Zeus backed off and sat on his haunches in front of the man, ready to pounce if necessary. When Carlos got a good look at the man in the moonlight, he said, "I know you. You're around Bobo's desk quite often."

"Yeah, you've seen me."

"What's your name? What's your association with Bobo?"

"I might as well be straight. You've got me now. My name is Bobby Camacho, and I'm the guy that the hotels use for special requests."

Carlos looked inside the brown bag. It was filled with finely-combed marijuana, rolling papers and matches. "You mean drugs?"

"I do drugs, as well as lining up felines and setting up gambling games. I saw your friends yesterday at a game. They didn't seem to be interested in the dice or cards, but insinuated that they wanted a taste of drugs. The man had his woman with him, so the prosties were probably not on the shopping list."

He continued, "I talked it over with Bobo. He knew who your friends and where I could contact them privately after the luau, but it had to be fast, because they were returning to the Mainland. So I watched them leave the luau and decided to contact them on the beach."

Joy said, "You scared the hell out of us. We thought you were going to kill us."

"No, just make some sales for your trip home. Bobo said you two didn't smoke."

Bobby added, "Sorry, I knew you were worried when I saw you flying down the beach, your feet kicking up sand. You must be fast in the 100 meters."

Carlos and Johnny took Bobby Camacho back to the picnic tables and decided to gather what info they might develop. He had about a kilo of grass, enough to be busted for sales, and he knew it. Carlos asked, "This sales thing is not important to me but what about all the murders and disappearances. You got anything to do with that?"

"Hell no, I don't do anything violent or stupid. You could ask Bobo; he seems to know everything about what is happening on the island."

Carlos said, "See that barbeque fire over in the sand. I want you to walk over and throw the marijuana in the fire. Just get rid of it."

Bobby did as he was told. Tom had been checking the area where Bobby had come out of the jungle. He found Bobby's pack sack which contained a knife, three packages of condoms, and seven sex toys still wrapped in new store packaging.

When Tom approached the group, he asked, "What do you do with the condoms and sex toys. It appears that you're full service with dope and sex items?"

Bobby replied, "My customers always want the damnest things—so I give them what they want. Sex toys are always popular. The customers are away from home and just want to try something different, and if it's with an experienced prostie, the more fun they have. The condoms are just for safety."

Carlos laughed and said, "You be the man. Not only are you a provider, some might call you a procurer or pimp, but you are also concerned about STD's for your clients. You should get a reward for community service."

Tom asked, "What about the knife. It's a mean little weapon with a strong fixed blade, good for cutting throats."

"I just use it for self-defense. Some guys have tried to get my dope for free. Even had one guy try to rob me."

Carlos asked, "What do you know about the two guys killed in the parking lot."

"Hey man, don't try to pin that one on me. Everybody knows they had their throats cut, but it wasn't me."

Tom said, "I see some red stuff on the knife, looks like dried blood."

"I used it to kill a pig at my dad's house. You can call my dad—239-1271. He can verify that."

Tom replied, "And what should I say? This is Tom parker calling for your son. He's been selling drugs and he has knife with him that has dried blood on the blade. He said he didn't kill the two guys selling drugs in the hotel parking lot. He said he slaughtered a pig at your house. Can you please verify?"

"No, not like that! He already suspects I'm into something illegal. I've always have money but no job. I just tell him I get Social Security benefits for my lack of education."

"Or for being a dumb shit."

Bobby cast his eyes at the floor, and said, "I know. I should be in school. My mother tells me that about twice a week."

In his most serious voice, he queried, "I want to clear this up. Would you be willing to take a lie detector test right now?"

Behind Bobby, Carlos and Johnny were about to bust a cut, laughing inside. Carlos whispered to Johnny, "I'm about to develop a hernia—I think my guts are to going to spill out through my stomach wall." Tom saw them laughing and was barely able to control himself.

"You mean just about the knife or if I killed those guys?"

"Yep, I'm not interested in your other crimes or life style."

Bobby answered, "Okay then, what do I do?"

"I'm going to handcuff you behind your back. You have to pull your arms around your butt, and bring the handcuffs out in front." Tom had applied the cuffs tight, and every move that Bobby made would put put pressure on his wrists."

Bobby looked puzzled, "What does that prove?"

"It means if you are lying, your body will be tense, and you won't be able to get the cuffs to the front."

"Now, answer this question. Did you kill those guys in the parking lot?"

Bobby replied in the negative.

Tom said, "Go. Let's see if you're lying." Bobby was thin and tall.

Bobby made his moves, wiggling and trying to push his butt backwards through his cuffed arms, and to bring them up through his legs. Several times, he said, red-faced, "This is tough and it hurts."

Tom said, "The truth will prevail, or maybe you are lying and you won't be able to do it."

Bobby finally managed to maneuver the cuffs out in front. He let out a yell of accomplishment and said, "See, I did it. I told you I was telling the truth." His wrists were beginning to swell, and were likely bruised.

Tom said, "Yeah, you did it. I didn't believe you at first but the test proves you're telling the truth."

Bobby grimaced, "Maybe you can release the cuffs. My hands are starting to tingle, and they're really red and hot."

Tom yelled over at the laughing spectators, and said, "Bobby is telling us the truth. He didn't kill those guys in the parking lot."

Carlos said, "Now we're getting somewhere. At least we have one guy that tells the truth."

Tom took off the handcuffs.

Carlos said, "Time to talk to Bobo." He admonished Bobby not to talk to Bobo and tell him what had happened. He added, "If you call Bobo, I'll not only make it a personal mission to stop your drug sales, but I will also telephone your father. I know him through my extended family."

Bobby nodded that he understood. Carlos threw the items from the packsack into the fire, along with the knife that would burn down to a metal carcass.

Chapter 18

TIME TO TALK TO BOBO

Horoto and Johnny spoke to Bobo in their office the next day. It was being handled as a personnel matter. Carlos decided to sit in the background and mentally take notes.

Horoto and Johnny still hadn't decided to terminate Bob at this juncture, wanting to wait to hear more from him. They both knew that he offset a lot of the bureaucratic government hassles with regulations and licenses.

Horoto didn't waste time and got right to the problems. He said, "Bobo, you're been here a long time and overall did a good job. But we know you've been skimming money off the top, shorting the hotel on tours and dive trips, putting a make on the employee's shift and hours, and that you're the local godfather in all the vice activities, like dope, gambling and girls. You could probably make a fortune with just blackmailing your clients."

"After this meeting, we'll let you know about your work status. We're not getting the police involved right now because the chances are the clients don't want to be identified and testify in court. Am I right?"

Bobo responded, "I have many clients way up in government and business. There's no need to expose them—they're basically good people except for a few morality flaws, like most people." He added, "I might also mention some of the well-known women around the island would be embarrassed about some of their requests."

Johnny said, "We're not into prosecuting and persecuting anyone. If you stay aboard, we want you to clean up your act and get the rightful profits back to the hotel, not into your personal bank account. We also want to help clear up the missing persons from the hotel, and also find the bastard that killed Lucy."

Bobo said, "The information and gossip about the two dead guys in the parking lot is accurate. The crazy fools used to brag how they were ripping off the Chinese gangsters. I even tried to explain how the tongs worked, but they didn't listen, and you know what happened. I had very little action with those guys. They usually sold meth or heroin, and if you've investigated me, you know we only distribute marijuana. If fact, I supporting a campaign right now to legalize marijuana."

Johnny said, "If it's legal, it will cut into your profit margin."

"That's going to be okay. I need less money now. I dropped the teeny bopper—my wife said "me or her," not a tough choice. I have three kids with my wife, and she doesn't smoke or drink. The teeny was a lark and a lot of fun, but she still had a lot of growing up to do. When she didn't get her way, she got all whiny and bitchy. With her hot body, she'll find another sugar daddy real fast."

Carlos laughed and said, "Think of the money you'll save on cell phones and IPods."

"You are so right. Now, let's talk about Lucy, the Porno Queen."

Horoto asked, "What do you know about her death?"

"Not a whole lot. We were all shocked when that happened. Her partner that night wasn't booked through me, and we don't know who it was. It could have been a hundred guys and several women, or someone out of the disco. She made a lot of her dates while dancing and drinking. With Porno all you needed was a nice personality, a hundred bucks and bag of grass."

Horoto asked, "How about the Thompsons? They disappeared just before Porno's death."

"Again, I don't know about some of their associations. The people that have disappeared, like the Chinese couple, have not been my clients. Mostly I suppose they made contact in Garapan or another village, went with their instincts, and ran into someone sinister and deadly. Dopers all want to keep both the dope and the money. Life and death mean nothing to those losers." He continued, "Mostly these off-island dealers want meth and I don't get close to those skinny freaks. They get all weird and are completely unpredictable."

Carlos asked, "What do you now about the Japanese jogger, the lady who taught aerobics at our hotel?"

"Again, nothing. That seemed to be a random thing with the lady jogging at night. The beach trail lights have not been lighted up lately because of a power shortage. She had driven in from her apartment in San Vicente, left her car at the Oleai Beach Club and then jogged up to the DFS area. She just disappeared into thin air. She wasn't reported missing until about 3:00 AM by her roommate. Her car was still in the parking lot at the trailhead. Apparently it hadn't been broken into."

Horoto asked, "What do you know about the thirty unsolved murders in the past ten years?"

"Again, not much. I'm not being elusive. The only ones that involved our hotel were the two missing housekeepers, both from the Philippines and about twenty-one years old. This was their first overseas job and they had only been with us about six months."

"What were the circumstances on them?"

"They had a late dinner at the employee's cafeteria and told the other workers that they were tired and ready for bed. They shared a small room together. When they didn't report for work at six o'clock next morning, their supervisor went to the employee barracks and when he received no answer to his knocking, he opened the door with his passkey, and discovered that they were gone. There was no forced entry and their apartment hadn't been disturbed."

Johnny asked, "Did the police develop any leads?"

"*Nada*. The other missing persons or homicides had the same results. Most of them involved foreign workers or outer islanders with no relatives on Saipan. A few involved domestic violence where it was the old case of the wife 'slipping and falling' off a cliff while the couple was fishing or exploring caves. Never any witnesses of course. The police never did any follow-up on the conditions and relationships in the marriages—never suggested polygraphs."

Johnny inquired, "Find any bodies?

"None of course. Usually the 'falls' took place where the sharks like to search for their dinners in the ocean sanctuaries. There are many ocean points that the sharks cleanse the waters by chewing up any carrion, human or otherwise."

"That could account for some of our missing people?"

"Sure but there's no telling for certain." He questioned any conclusion, "Or maybe the women disappeared on their own and were skipping out on large credit card bills. In both those cases, there was no legal marriage, just common law. There were no children involved, and possibly the couple met up in Guam or Hawaii, and then opened accounts in the husband's name."

"Much mystery here. It's too bad the cops never did any work on these cases."

Bobo laughed, "Ya gotta make time for coffee, and if there's any time left, head over to the girlfriend's house."

"Possibly we should hire someone with clairvoyant powers, like a psychic."

Bobo suggested, "I don't know any psychics but I could find you a witch doctor out in a remote village."

Johnny chuckled, "Mahalo for your honesty and information. We'll let you know by tomorrow if you will be staying on the payroll."

"Don't worry, I'll get with the program, and you won't regret giving me a second chance." Carlos noted that he was a charmer and had a million-dollar smile, the perfect salesman. It was no wonder that he was successful in his deviousness.

They all shook hands and Bobo left for his desk in the lobby. Horoto said, "Best count your fingers after shaking with that fellow. Make sure there's ten left."

Carlos said, "He looked hurried. Maybe was losing out on lucrative deals at his desk."

Johnny asked, "What do you guys think about keeping him around."

Horoto said, "Old Japanese saying, 'let your friends wander but keep your enemies close at hand.' I say keep him on a short leash."

Johnny agreed, as did Carlos.

Chapter 19

TO THE FAR REACHES
OF MICRONESIA

Activities and events were generally going well at both the Californian and Beach Hotels. The tourist trade from Japan was slow; the tsunami had taken its toll on the economy and the people were still mourning the loss of their people. However, the numbers of customers were picking up from Russia, Taiwan and China. Most of the hotels on Saipan were operating at 80% occupancy, which was stimulating for the lagging economy.

Johnny and Jan Nan had found time to slip off and see some of the outer Micronesian islands like Palau, Pohnpei and Chuuk. They also had a chance to discover each other, and soon there was a deep affection developing for one another. Commitment came up several times, even marriage, but Jan Nan was hesitant. Her marriage had been unpleasant—she was so excited when she got the opportunity to work outside of her little town in China but the husband wasn't—he wanted a traditional stay-at-home wife. She had had two relationships since—one with an American, who liked to keep his options open, and a Japanese man who was overbearing and demanding, and a detailest about everything from the kitchen to the bedroom.

Johnny was a new experience for her. To her, he was the modern man, sensitive, intelligent and masculine all rolled into a complete package. He asked her opinion on just about everything—he included her in his life, and she did the same. Probably what enthralled her above everything else—he was happy and carefree and adventuresome. He was just about willing to try anything new. She had always heard that nerdy men thought only about computers and video games.

So they took diving lessons and explored the wrecks in Truk Lagoon. The Japanese fleet had been caught in the lagoon by American bombers and dozens of ships were sunk and hundreds of Japanese sailors killed. Since 1944, the sunken ships had formed their own colorful mini-reefs, and tropical fish and octopuses were spotted in the wrecks and throughout the lagoon. It was a diver's paradise and always recognized as one of the top dive sports in the entire world. It was good that the underwater ghost ships were protected by law as a National Monument.

They flew to Pohnpei and enjoyed the local, exotic dancing and jungle treks. They learned to drink *sakau,* a local hypnotic brew made from roots and pepper leaves, and climbed the highest mountain on Pohnpei, which has 400+ inches of rain per year, and the water slides down the mountain in rushing rivers with bright, clear waterfalls. It was a spiritual journey into mist-covered jungle forests with giant ferns and friendly people in remote villages. Marijuana abounded—it was easy to grow, and imported beer had become very expensive. So they learned to smoke grass and drink sakau, and spent many an afternoon basking in the sun listening to old cassettes of Michael Jackson and Jimmy Buffet.

On their last Micronesian stop, they deplaned on Palau for several days, and experienced boat trips through the Rock Islands and visited the massive oyster beds. They made a mountain hike to see the fresh water lake that had thousands of jellyfish without stingers. Jan Nan taught Johnny how to use chopsticks and enjoy sushi and sashimi with a touch of wasabi. During this period, they had become intimate lovers. They had gotten to the point of discussing the future as a couple and even marriage was mentioned, this time by Jan Nan.

By the last day of their journey, they flew from Palau to Guam and had to wait for two hours for their flight home to Saipan. Jan Nan brought up the topic of exploring a divorce in China. She halfway expected Johnny to pull back, divorce of the old and the marriage as the new are serious steps, especially for a bachelor like Johnny who had never married. But he didn't flinch and gave her the go-ahead with a wide smile. She made it clear that she had a child, 14-year-old Sun Hee (commonly called Sunny by Westerners), and would like the child to join them so she could finish her schooling in American institutions.

Johnny said, "And how could I refuse anything from my darling woman."

"Oh, you sweet man. I will slave, cook and make love with you."

Laughing, Johnny replied, "We are so full of sugar that we'll drive our friends crazy back home with jealousy."

"Or they'll go into diabetic shock with the syrup. We'll be like an old married people after several weeks."

"Or months or years."

Chapter 20

GREGORIO SANTOS CAPTURED

Johnny watched the passengers separate at the boarding area. He looked over at two Guam uniformed policemen and a large fellow in a business suit, likely a federal agent, escorting a local man to the plane. He said, "It appears we've got a bad guy traveling with us, heading for jail and a trial no doubt."

"Should we take another flight?"

"No, no problem. He'll he handcuffed and his feet chained, and he's got a professional-looking guy escorting him."

Johnny chatted among the other passengers and soon learned that the prisoner was Gregorio Santos, the alleged killer of the Japanese jogger that had taught aerobics and dance at the Californian Hotel. He appeared harmless and meek, not a vicious-appearing criminal. He was a skinny little emaciated man in need of grooming and a bath. He appeared, from what Johnny had seen on television and read in magazine, like a typical meth user. When he turned, he saw that Gregorio had terrible, ugly teeth, probably from rotting and falling out if he was the cooker in the meth lab.

Johnny called Carlos and let him know that one of the bad guys had been nabbed, and that he would be arriving in about an hour. The feds were bringing him back from Palau. It was a FBI case because the victim was Japanese, and the suspect had crossed state lines to escape prosecution. Carlos felt better knowing that the suspect was in custody with the FBI and would probably go to trial in federal court without major mistakes and interference from the local AG's office.

The trip back to Saipan was uneventful. The FBI agent left with the Saipan police to make sure that the suspect got booked correctly into the local jail.

Over the course of the next few days, Carlos talked to Agent Dan Simpson and got the scoop on the arrest of Gregorio. The FBI, like many professional law enforcement agencies, uses a series of informants to get to the big guys. Gregorio was considered a big guy in terms of his violations. So when a meth user was busted by the Guam Police, they picked up general details, informed Dan who dropped everything to capture this guy. The little jerk's supplier was Gregorio who cooked his own poison in the Guam Hills.

Dan drew some 'buy' money for the informant and worked out a series of contacts. Dan figured if it wasn't the wanted murderer, at least they would have some good dope buys that the Guam Police could follow up on. But as luck sometimes happens, the seller was Gregorio Santos. The informant was wired, made his buy and skedaddled, and a dozen cops pounced on Gregorio. He offered no resistance.

Gegorio's only statement after hearing his Miranda Rights was simple, "What took you guys so long?"

There is no death penalty for murder on Saipan. The crime didn't apply to the death penalty under the categories in the federal laws for terrorism and treason. Gregorio knew this and wasn't about to confess or plead guilty, until he started to withdraw from the drugs.

Carlos joined Dan who said, "Come clean with us, and we'll get you a medical treatment other than an aspirin from a jail nurse. It's up to you."

Gregorio answered with a series of expletives. Dan replied, "Okay then. We'll see you tomorrow . . . or not."

Carlos said, "Bad words, bad attitude."

"He'll come around. He's just another dumb-ass doper. The withdrawal is tough stuff."

Several hours later, Dan and Carlos were watching the lavender sunset disappear into the Philippines Sea, and smoking a Filipino dark tobacco cigar. Dan's cell phone rang. It was a corrections officer at the jailhouse who told him that Gregorio wanted to talk. Dan said, "Just tell him I'll see him right after breakfast in the morning."

The officer said, "He won't be happy. He's been moaning and groaning for over an hour."

Dan replied, "So be it. I'll see you folks in the morning."

Next morning, Dan and Carlos had breakfast at the Beach Hotel. You could smell the fresh baked bread and cinnamon fifty yards from the kitchen. It was just another fantastic culinary morning delight—Guangman had the typical Western choices, like bacon, sausage, eggs and hashed brown potatoes but also had prepared fresh mango juice, banana bread and pudding, and his world-famous cinnamon rolls.

Dan said, "I'll be 300 pounds if I'm around Guangman much longer."

Carlos replied, "Just a long stroll this evening along the beach. Burn off the fat. The sand make you work harder, plus spiritually your soul will glow with the sunset colors. Horizontal dancing is a real weight-reducer and fun too."

"Good idea. Now, I want you to come with me to the jail. You know these characters and how their minds work."

Carlos said, "You know as well as I do but I'll be glad to tag along. The guy will want out so he can score more dope, and also he'll betray his relatives, including his own mother, and friends to get there."

"For sure, I have a good bargaining chip, but he's not going anywhere except to the courthouse."

"He'll settle for prescribed drugs while he coming down from whatever planet he was visiting. Let's head over to the jail to see what he has to say."

Dan and Carlos checked into the jailhouse.

Heading for the attorneys' area in the jail, Raffy Rodriquez and Carlos passed one another in the hallway. Neither acknowledged the other.

A jailer brought Gregorio Santos to the interview room. He was a wreck. If possible, it looked like he had lost more weight.

Dan said, "This is Carlos Montano—he's working the case with me. I've already told you about your Miranda Rights—up to you if you wanna talk to us."

"Yeah, I do. I know my rights—I've heard them so many that I could recite them back to you. I wanna clear this thing up and change my life. I'm dying fast."

Dan exclaimed, "Then let's get going. I have my tape recorder with me." Dan recited the date and time, and introduced Carlos, and then Gregorio, explaining why they were to talking to him.

After about twenty minutes about his criminal background. Dan asked point-blank if he had killed the Japanese jogger, Horomi Toguchi.

"She was just on the street one night when I needed money for drugs. I didn't mean to kill her—I just wanted her wallet and money. I could see a bulge inside her running shorts on her right hip. Later on, I discovered that the bulge was her damn cell phone. She wasn't carrying money and wasn't wearing any jewelry, not even a cheap watch."

He continued, "I grabbed her and tried to throw her inside my truck, but she struggled. She was physically fit and very strong and wiry. In the fight, I wrapped my hands around her throat and squeezed hard. There was a loud crack—I think I broke her neck. Suddenly she went limp, and it was over. I tried to revive her but she was dead."

Carlos asked, "What happened then?"

"I tried not to panic and pushed her on the floor boards of my truck. She was tiny, maybe ninety pounds, and fit down easily on the floor. No one had seen us along the beach. I drove around, trying to figure out what to do with her body. I ended up at the dump; you know the landfill in Marpi? She was light-weight, so I lifted her out of the truck and threw her over the fence. I got a shovel out of my truck, jumped the fence, and dug a grave for her on the far end of the landfill."

Dan frowned, "Did you rape her?"

"No, no way. I was too stressed out to do anything. It wasn't a sex killing for me—it was a robbery that went sour." He paused and added, "I was so stupid."

Dan asked, "Are you going to show us where she buried, or do we have to dig up the whole landfill? We have to verify the location and also get her body back to her parents in Japan. They are very distressed."

Gregorio answered, "Yeah, I'll show you but first I want some withdrawal drugs and something for pain. My whole body is fighting, deciding to live or die."

"We'll come back in two days. Meanwhile, I'll have the jail doctor see you and possibly prescribe some drugs. That's not my call. How's that sound?"

"Good."

Dan asserted, "Don't change your mind because you feel better after drugs and a decent meal. Keep in mind you wanna clear up this whole mess, and our report will indicate cooperation from you, which will look good for you on the court record."

"No, man. I won't change. I've hit bottom—only way is up . . . or death."

True to his word a few days later, Gregorio said that he would show Carlos and Dan where the body was. His haggard face was starting to fill out, and his skin color was now almost normal, rather than showing the see-through death pallor. He agreed that the Medical Examiner could come along, along with two strong gravediggers who would do the physical labor and load the body into the heavy plastic black bag. Although the grave was already covered over with grass and weeds, it was easy to find. The ground had given away from the recent rains, and it was now recessed with the body dissipating.

Carlos took a video recording of the process. Once the digging started, Gregorio was placed back in a secure federal car. The body was only a few deet down, and was easily dug up. It had been raining so the soil hadn't turned into hard adobe. The body was still dressed in jogging clothes. Most of her flesh had disintegrated. Carlos recognized a little purse tied to her right running shoe—it was her identification tag if she even collapsed or got hurt on a run. Carlos opened it. It was Horomi; she could be positively identified by her DNA matching up with her parents.

As it developed, DNA wasn't necessary. Her parents brought her dental charts to Saipan, and two of the local dentists, Doctors Markon and White, after reviewing the charts, confirmed that it was definitely Hiromi.

Gregorio was arraigned in federal court and given a public defender. The negotiations opened between the prosecutor and the defense for a guilty plea. Gregorio didn't want to go in front of a jury for a trial. This went back and forth for six months, finally with Gregorio pleading guilty for a twenty-five year sentence in federal prison. Hopefully Gregorio would experience drug rehabilitation and some schooling. There were unlikely chances of parole for his crime, so the island wouldn't be seeing and worrying about Gregorio for a long stretch. When he got out of prison, he would be too old to be robbing and murdering tourists. By this time, his sense of excitement would include a television and a lazy boy chair, or a book if he had learned to read.

Dan gave a complete briefing to Horomi's family. They went to the gravesite, lighted candles and incense, and prayed for her for several hours. Many people in the Japanese community joined in. The officials transferred her body from the morgue to Guam where she was cremated and readied for his homeward bound plane to Japan. She was the only child in the Toguchi Family.

Johnny sent the family her personal belongings and her last paycheck, and five thousand dollars to cover her transportation and funeral expenses, He also sent along her employee plaques—she had been voted "Outstanding Employee" for two years running.

One year later, as part of Gregorio's rehabilitation or maybe he had developed a conscience and sensitivity to others, he wrote a letter of apology and regrets to the Toguchi Family. They never answered.

Chapter 21

THE MYSTERIOUS GAMBLER RETURNS

Tom Parker called and asked Johnny if he could take a VIP overflow guest for one of the penthouses at The Californian. The Beach Hotel was filled up by a Korean Tupper-Ware conference, ladies in pink everywhere. Johnny said that there was an extra penthouse available.

Tom said, "This fellow's name is Han Gaozu and he travels with an entourage consisting of his mistress Mang Zhao, his bodyguard Simi Quian and his driver/handyman Cao Cao. He's Chinese and loves to gamble at the casino on Tinian. He also likes to play tennis. I can ask our tennis pro, Jonah Reese, to help out at your courts. I saw you had your four courts re-surfaced."

Johnny responded, "Anything else we should know?"

"Well, I'll just say he's one mysterious character. He's a good-looking guy and Mang is the beauty of all beauties. He's quiet, low profile, and travels with a lot of cash. He won't want a receipt at your hotel for anything—just pays cash every where he goes."

Johnny asked, "Any chance of counterfeit. What do you think he's into?"

"No problem, his money is the real McCoy. I never saw him doing anything illegal. They smoke a little grass but nothing hard. We just assume he's laundering money at the casino but we don't know for sure. They're good guests—no problems of any kind."

"When do they get here?"

Tom chuckled and said, "They love to surprise us. They're in the air right now flying in from Guam."

"We'll be ready. How do they get to Tinian for the gambling?"

Tom answered, "Bobo can handle it. They'll charter a private plane to take them back and forth. Money won't be a problem."

"That's only a ten-minute flight. Do they have the pilot just hang out until they're finished playing?"

"Han will pay the 'wait time.' He even gave the last pilots two hundred bucks a day to play with at the casino, but no drinking."

Within an hour, Han and his entourage were at the front desk. During registration, Isabella, the desk clerk, asked for a credit card to keep on file. Han grunted, "What's that for?"

Isabella answered, "It's just routine. We keep the card just in case of pilferage, damage, or to pay for restaurant and bar bills."

Han seemed offended, so Horoto stepped forward and added, "All the guests are required to do it. It isn't a personal issue."

Han said something to the effect, "Hurrumph." He looked at Simi and directed, "Give the lady five thousand dollars. That should hold us for a few days. I don't use credit cards." When Simi opened his briefcase, Horoto noticed that it was loaded with stacks of one hundred bills.

Bobo sensed a financial opportunity fresh at hand, and scurried about loading all their cases and bags onto to the luggage cart and showed them to their 3-bedroom penthouse. It was to Han's liking, with a large lanai and an endless view.

Han made arrangements with Bobo for the private plane to shuttle the group to Tinian for their games of blackjack, baccarat, and craps. Han also asserted that he would be playing in a high-stakes poker tournament. Han asked that a five-course meal be delivered to their penthouse at two in the morning every night, and that he line up a few hours of tennis with Jonah at twelve noon. He requested a beach run and a personal trainer at about 10 o'clock and then he explained that liked to play tennis in the heat of the day.

Han slipped five Ben Franklins to Bobo and asserted, "Get me what I need and there will be more. Right now, I need you to take Mang up to Garapan and help her score about fifty sticks of grass."

Bobo knowing the new rules said, "I can't buy her any dope by hotel policy. But I can show her where to go and make sure that she doesn't get ripped off."

"Just take her to the spot. She knows how to buy."

Their custom schedule went on for four days—run, tennis, lunch, rest, casino, late room service. Han gave Bobo five hundred bucks a day to make sure everything went smoothly. Bobo didn't see any illegal activity but he noticed the pile of money in the briefcase was getting smaller and smaller. They didn't have any suspicious characters coming to their room, especially the dope-dealer types, and they barely smoked any grass. Simi and Cao had a few late-night female visitors during their stay. That was discreetly done with no loud noises or drunken noisy ladies screaming in delight.

Han and his entourage remained a mystery. The staff was tipped handsomely and Han saw that Jonah received an extra hundred dollars besides his daily rate for lessons.

The departure date was organized and automatic, even though it was their first stay at the Californian. When Simi opened the briefcase to reconcile the closing bill, Horoto noted that the briefcase was basically empty. The greenbacks had either been lost at the high-stakes games, or the money was now circulating in the USA financial system . . . or maybe tucked way with some off-shore secret bank.

Han and his entourage left quietly, and it was like they had never been there. Johnny called Tom and asked, "What's your take on those folks?"

"Did they pay their bill?"

"Yep, with cash. Legitimate currency."

"Cause any damage? Murder anybody?"

"No problems . . . good guests."

Tom chuckled and said, "Samo here. They've been at our hotel twice. I was hoping you could explain their angle. Except for the money-laundering possibility, Carlos and I still have no idea."

Johnny said, "At this rate, we may never drop the 'mystery hotel' handle."

Tom laughed again, "Not our job to sort out our guests . . . but it is our job to provide service, be profitable and put their bucks in the bank."

"Mission accomplished."

Chapter 22

ANOTHER TALK WITH
RAFFY RODRIQUEZ

Raffy called from the jail phone and said that he needed to talk to Carlos about some "insurance matters." When Carlos arrived the next day, he was told that Raffy had been a disciplinary problem and they had locked him in isolation with no visitors allowed. Both he and Tom parker had Private Investigator licenses but the jailer wouldn't budge to make an exception to allow Carlos to enter.

Carlos called Special Agent Dan Simpson and asked him for help. He couldn't imagine that the jail would turn away an FBI agent. But they did, and there was an order which stated that any contact with Raffy had to be cleared with the Commissioner. The officer and the supervisor were both being typical bureaucratic jerks. Raffy must have had some good scoop and the bad guys/criminals knew it.

Carlos arranged for a lawyer, a former US Marshall, to represent Raffy and request an interview about his crimes and a pending appeal. The Marshall, Clyde Titus, hired Carlos as his private investigator to handle follow-up on any of Raffy's cases.

On the first trip to interview Raffy, Carlos was turned away. The jailer said he needed a court order. However, Clyde got to the interview room and the guards escorted Raffy from the isolation cell. He was a mess—dirty clothes, filthy body, and bumps and bruises on his face and shoulders. Clyde asked the jailer what had happened.

The jail replied, "I can't talk about it. All the information and questions must be handled by the Commissioner or his spokesperson, who happens to be the governor's lackey . . . I mean his nephew." He paused and said, "Forget I said anything."

Clyde reminded him that he was the jailer and therefore, responsible for the conditions of his prisoners. "No, I can't forget about it. This isn't communist Cuba. If you went to corrections school, you know you have to treat prisoners fairly and humanely, and if not, you'll be doing your own stint in the federal pen." He added, "If you keep acting like an uneducated fool, and if you so desire, we can send this situation to several agencies about the mistreatment of prisoners, most significantly being the FBI."

The jailer, a nice clean-cut young man, shuttered and said, "Man, don't do this to me. I need the job. My wife just had a baby last month."

"I'm not after you. I just want the bigwigs in this matter, and my investigator is trying to find several killers."

"Okay then, can I just give you a little info? You can get the rest from Raffy."

"Depends on what you give me."

"My tape recorder is off, and I know the hidden camera and recorder have been disabled in this room. Now, what have you got?"

Nervously, the jailer said that some of the supervisors had heard that Raffy was talking to Carlos about some deadly stuff that happened at the hotel."

"And?"

"They said to get Raffy and beat it out of him about what he knew. Raffy didn't talk so he was worked over by a sergeant. I didn't hit him."

Clyde accused, "But you held him, right? And you saw it happen?"

"I'm afraid so. I didn't want to cross the sergeant."

"OK, you can go now before the other jailers squeal on you to the sergeant." He asked, "How far up the food chain does this thing go?"

"According to the jail scuttlebutt, all the way to the top. It's about drugs and the murder of the girl they call the Porno Queen."

"Keep your mouth closed. Leave Raffy with me. But afterwards get him some food. You understand?"

The jailer nodded and left quietly.

Clyde said to Raffy, "They wouldn't let Carlos in but I assure that you can trust me. I'm not part of any clique or family group. There not many of us Detroit types out here in the islands—that's my home town."

Raffy said, "Here's what I wanted to tell Carlos. The governor, several senators and a few directors visited Porno in the past. They also smoked some grass with her—she wouldn't allow any hard drugs. The other girl that OD'd was a favorite and they often used 'ice' with her. Who actually did the killing, that I don't know. But the people I mentioned are rumored to have been regulars and Bobo knows about it. He'll play innocent, but his fingers are in just about everything."

"Anyone, anything specific?'

"So far, rumors and innuendoes. I did overhear one of the jailers saying that he had laid the governor's squeeze several times. His name is Roberto Garcia—you might get something out of him. He definitely likes to brag."

Clyde turned on his cell phone and took a dozen photos of Raffy displaying his injuries. He called in the jailer and let him know that he had the photos and didn't expect there would be additional "interrogations." He added, "I don't want to hear about any accidental falls in the shower or some weird story about resisting arrest or some drug overdose. If any of this gets out of control and beyond your level, give me a call, day or night. Here's my card." The jailer slipped it in his pocket.

The jail sergeant appeared, and he vehemently said, "You have to leave now. I don't care if you're a lawyer, your time is up. Time to go!"

Clyde and Carlos stopped off at the FBI headquarters and downloaded the photos onto Dan's computer. They filled him in the beatings and threats. Dan took copious notes.

Dan said, "Based on this information, I'm going to get a court order releasing him to my custody. We can keep him safe in the Guam jailhouse. Unfortunately the closest federal jails are in California."

Carlos said, "You have to move fast before Raffy has that "accidental fall."

Dan grimaced, "That I well know. I lost an effective informant in the Los Angeles Jail by waiting to the next day. He was shanked while exercising in the yard."

Carlos smiled, "Gracias, Muchacho. I know Raffy will appreciate staying alive."

Dan spoke to the federal prosecutor, showed him the photos, and received a high priority court order allowing the FBI to seize control of Raffy for allegations of violations of civil rights and transport him to Guam. Raffy and Dan got on the last plane to Guam for the night.

Dan had called Carlos with the information and he, Carlos and Raffy had a chat at the airport in a private interview room before the flight. Again, Dan took piles of notes, and the new phone photographs indicated that Raffy hadn't been beaten again.

After the interview, Carlos spoke to Johnny in the parking lot. "This caper is as big as we imagined. Raffy gave us a list of the names that visited Porno, and how much marijuana they had ordered from Bobo, not just for using with Porno but enough for "a take-out" in the proverbial brown paper-bag. He also mentioned a few names that might be involved in the OD case involving Katrina, the Russian gal."

Chapter 23

BOBO AGAIN

To the best of everyone's knowledge, Bobo had turned into an honest employee, with tons of written and verbal information about making the hotel more profitable and attractive to guests. Bosses were watching his every move. His longtime job depended on it. Entering Johnny's office, Bobo was immaculate wearing his blue shorts and flowery aloha shirt. He brushed his hair back with his right hand—this didn't necessarily indicate nervousness but was a well-known idiosyncrasy of his.

Carlos said, "Bobo, no time for games and a runaround. This time we have names and dates. We're going to go over the OD Russian gal and the Porno Queen step by step."

Johnny declared, "No more dope from you of any kind. If they have to use drugs, they can go on the streets and get their own. Also you are not to be doing any pimping for anyone, and no more free rooms and free room service, or any kind of illegal activity. Got it?"

"I understand. Rules and laws are to be followed."

"Now, who was the room with the Russian girls when Katrina overdosed? We have some information but we want to hear it from you. No sense in lying or fudging the truth."

"The guy that set the deal up for the two senators, one from Rota and one from Guam—not sure who they are for certain. I never asked names."

"Then who was the guy, the go-between?"

"That was a gopher kind of character. He does a little of this, and a little that. His name is Gus Gonzales. He's kinda of a shadowy character—travels back and forth from Guam. When he isn't around, I call a guy named Ricardo in Yigo on Guam. The Guam politicians like to come over here for their womanizing and rendezvous activities. No one knows them here. They supposedly come over for a bunco training or a liaison with our local politicos. The taxpayers get to pay for their fun. Of course, our politicos go over there. Makes for a nice arrangement. They get per diem money to spend, and also it keeps the wives from getting too suspicious."

"What happened that night with Katrina and the OD?"

"The senator from Guam brought over a package of heroin and another of ice that had been manufactured in Japan. The drugs were supposed to be strong and of high quality. No one had told the girls that. The four of them got high on small doses, but when the men went out to go fishing, Katrina helped herself to a death dose. It was way over-the-limit strong and she killed herself."

"The investigating cops, led by senior detective Felix Cabrera, at the scene called the senators by cell phone, and told them to stay away. They did and haven't been back since. Apparently all their items left in the room were disposed of by the cops, and the surfaces were wiped clean. By the time the cops finished, there was no evidence that they had ever been in the penthouse. Also, they were not officially booked in, the senators and the girls, so there' no written documentation of any kind."

"Did they hurt Olga, the cops?"

"It wasn't a big thing for her. They did her individually in the other bedroom. She was just happy to survive and not be hauled off to some dark jungle and left in a shallow grave. They told her that if she talked and made a complaint, she would be cut up and left for the pigs."

"She can be anonymous. I just need some info. Where can we find her?"

Bobo said, "She's long gone back to Tomsk, Russia. She told me that she was willing to endure the cold winters of Siberia, rather than being killed on a Pacific Island by some drunken politician. She also said that she had to leave because drugs and alcohol were getting the best of her."

Carlos asked, "Do you have a forwarding address or phone number for her?"

"Nope. We evened up our bills and fees to one another and off she went. I know she left because one of her friends came in to see about getting some "extra" work."

Johnny asked, "And my good man, what did you tell her?"

"I followed our policy to the letter. I said I was no longer in that kind of work. Told the same thing to Max who came in trying to sell some home-grown MJ."

Carlos said, "Good, now tell me about Porno. What happened with her?"

Regretfully he said, "She should never have died and been treated the way she ended up. If truth be known, she was a sweet, simple girl, but her sex drive and inner demons drove her to do risky stuff. I really liked her and felt extremely sad when she passed. I knew her more of like a father figure than a part-time lover." His limpid gaze met Carlos straight on. He added, "You know what I mean . . . right?"

Carlos said, "It's no secret. I visited Porno during my bachelor days. It's like Bobo says, 'she was a flat-out nice person.—she was happy and delightful.' But we separated when I met Daisy, my wife. But I have nothing critical to say about her, except we discussed her life style and what might result. She was fascinated by power and celebrity, so she often found herself tangled up with musicians and politicians, searching for a real relationship. It never worked out. To them, she was just a plaything. Bad combination—all of it."

"So who killed her, or left the drugs for the overdose? The Medical Examiner said that she died from an overdose, but it would rather difficult to shoot herself up and then tie herself to the four corner posts, plus she had massive bleeding and bruising in her pelvic area and on her breasts. No semen was saved for DNA analysis and matchup."

"This is a big scandal—it'll be all over the papers and TV."

"So?"

"Several people think it was the governor. But not so; it was his eldest son, Isaiah. He had this thing about S & M. He kept it under control most of the time, but he went wacko on several women in the past and with Porno."

Horoto concluded, "Very sensitive. How do we proceed? The local cops won't do anything except stall and interfere."

Carlos said, "The only thing we can do is go to the FBI and indicate drugs, fraud, and corruption from the governor on down and incompetence by the police. When no one claimed her body, she wasn't buried in the pauper's cemetery. The cops had her cremated and her ashes dumped at sea. There's no re-examination of the body possible now."

Horoto said, "This is one peculiar paradise. Crooked politicians and Yakuza."

Carlos summarized, "Porno is gone but I intend to bring her back to life for the case, and bring the killers to justice. We'll just re-construct her with every little piece of information we can find."

And Horoto-san, the little Samurai, exclaimed, "Hai!"

Chapter 24

DAN AND THE FEDS

Again, Dan Simpson and his fellow agents were glad to assist in the investigation. Cooperation from the feds was par for the course. Dan indicated that a check on Isaiah revealed that he had been in trouble on the Mainland for several counts of domestic violence, two for assault in various bars, and twice for the solicitation of a prostitute. The reports indicated that he particularly liked "rough sex" and he was willing to pay extra. One lady of the night had him arrested for battery in the bedroom but later dropped the charges. It was rumored that she had been paid off by one of the governor's cronies.

Figuring the Porno incident had settled down, he returned to Saipan and was spotted several times in the Garapan bars. There were several lightweight warrants out for Isaiah's arrest. The FBI had several reliable informants in the jailhouse. So they decided to arrest him on a Friday, trusting that he might stay in jail over the weekend before he posted bail or could be arraigned on Monday morning. The FBI snitches were both doing year-long sentences and knew their way around the jail and how everything worked. They were there 24/7 while the guards were only there generally forty hours a week. One of the informants, Micah, ended up in the same cellblock and day room, and Isaiah, not being able to control his mouth, started bragging about all the women he had scored with. He considered himself quite "the ladies man."

In his stories, the women were begging for it, and of course, he never had to pay. Typical macho chatter in the slammer.

Micah asked, "What happens if they turn you down?"

"I'm on them full force, and they can't resist me. I even give 'em drugs."

Micah smiled and said, "Hey Man, I've been around. There's always some bitch that says 'no way.' What do you do with her?"

"She's bought the farm, Man She's going down. No one can resist Isaiah."

"Did you ever take someone down all the way?"

His glare hardened, "I've had to do it once or twice. I'd do it again. Ya gotta teach the bitches whose boss."

Micah laughed and asked, "Any body I know, so I'll avoid her next time?"

"You've heard of her, Man. She's famous. She was called the Porno Queen at one of the hotels. I did her until she died."

Micah said, "I get out in about a year. I was fantasizing about doing her—I heard that she's dynamite!"

"Too late now. She's dead!"

Micah flung back his head and laughed loudly. "Dude, you are so full of shit, you're liable to blow up any minute. You're all talk; you never did the nasty with her!"

Isaiah jumped up from the bench and grabbed Micah around the neck. He asserted, "I did her. Not only in the romance department, but I killed her ass with drugs."

"Hey, let me go! I can hardly breathe. Man, you are intense, now I believe you. Whatever you say!"

Isaiah said, "Believe it, Man. You won't be screwing her any time soon. She's gone to whore heaven."

Isaiah bragged about how many women he had been with. He also said that he had to share Porno with his father and several political bigwigs. Sometimes he locked in a definite date with Porno through Bobo, but most of the time it just took a phone call, and she was ready for him. He paid her several hundred bucks each time plus kept her in a steady supply of marijuana. Occasionally she would try a few other drugs but very little at a time. He added that the night she died, after tying her up, he had shot her up with heroin and ice. He said that she squirmed for awhile and when she started to scream, he filled her mouth with her panties. After that, she went limp, she spasmed, and died. He said that he left the penthouse real fast after erasing all signs that he had been there.

Micah met clandestinely next day with Dan. Needing a minor collaboration of Micah's information for courtroom requirements, Dan and Carlos met with Bobo about setting up Isaiah with Porno. Bobo was obviously nervous about providing any info about the governor and his family. After explaining what he needed, Dan said, "Up to you, Bobo. We can drag you in front of the Grand Jury, and if you lie there, you'll be charged with perjury if you're caught in any misrepresentation and also for lying to a federal officer."

Bobo looked at Carlos and asked, "How about my job? This all happened before we had our talk."

Carlos said, "You had a fresh starting point after we talked. Now it's up to you if you going on with a clean slate, or intend to keep lying and handing out more BS."

Bobo glanced at Dan and said, "Well, here goes. I hope you guys can protect me or get me into a witness protection for the sake of my family." He hesitated and then said, "Yeah, I set up Isaiah and his father, the governor, about twenty times. The governor was usually fast, in and out of the penthouse in an hour, while Isaiah often spent the entire night. Some of their political friends also made visits, also some of the local bigshots."

Dan asked, "What else?"

"Sometimes after a date with Isaiah, Lucy would visit me next morning and say 'never again.' She often added, 'He is one loco bastard. He even brought a whip and lashed me while I was on the floor trying to get away. Even now I can hardly sit down on my bottom.' She wanted me to avoid a date whenever possible. That worked sometimes because I said that she already had a client. But one time, he went up to her room and there was no one there. He came back down and said that if I didn't cooperate and fix it up with Porno, he would tell the hotel management and the newspapers about my arrangements. He threatened by saying, 'If you think this hotel has a bad rep now, wait until I start telling everybody.' I didn't want to take a chance, so I explained everything to Lucy, and we just stalled him as much as possible."

"The date in question, the night she died. Did you set that one up?"

"Yeah, I unfortunately did. I keep a little memory booklet so I can keep track of who owes me money. That night is probably in the book. Isaiah paid me $100 that time for the hook-up, and promised to give $300 to Lucy."

Carlos said, "Go get it. I just want to look at the pertinent dates. Your other notes are your past business actions."

Bobo left to get his book, and Dan said, "This guy ripped you folks off and you're keeping him on the staff? He ought to be in the grey-bar hotel."

"It's a long story, but Johnny decided the good outweighs the bad. So far, he has once again become a good employee. That guy knows everything and everybody; and especially how to get past all the roadblocks of doing business on this little island."

When Bobo returned, Dan noted the entry and the date. He said, "That's it. We got what I needed to back up what he blabbed to Micah."

Dan seized the book for evidence. Bobo frowned and started to object, but changed his mind. It now appeared that a lot of his previous loans and owed payments wouldn't have to be paid—no record.

Dan went to the federal court and had Micah released to the FBI for protective custody. He arranged for the US Marshall to move Micah to the Guam jail facility for doing his jail time. When booking Micah into the Guam jail, the corrections officer said, "You must have all kind of shit going on in that little rock. We have another one of your guys here in protective custody, keep-away from other prisoners status."

The Deputy Marshall replied, "It's only the beginning, my friend. More coming."

Dan and one of his fellow agents went to the Saipan jail and had Isaiah brought to the front booking counter. Dan asserted, "Isaiah, you are being charged with murder and your bail until we go to court is set at $100,000."

Isaiah brazenly answered, "That's not going to happen. My uncle is on the way to bail me out on my other charges. I'm being bailed out and I'm leaving."

"Sorry, you are now in federal custody; and you are not bailing out. It may be late in life for you, but you are now accountable for your behavior."

Even the corrections officers were aware of federal authority. He struggled but they forcefully pushed him back inside.

Dan said, "Stupid spoiled brat. Now he's has to face the truth for once in his life. Papa can't save his butt on this one."

"Unless they take out Bobo," Carlos quietly said.

"I assure you that they will not get him . . . but hopefully we'll get them, and soon."

Chapter 25

THE TROPICAL DOLDRUMS

Peace broke out on Saipan. Except for an occasional purse snatch from a Japanese tourist, it was staying calm and almost safe for a woman to walk the beach at twilight. Isaiah's murder case was working its way up on the court calendar, and the defense and prosecution were trying to reach a reasonable deal. He never made bail, and the island influences on getting him freed up on some technality or lost evidence hit a brick wall. Thank goodness for Uncle Sam and its' stalwart agents. J. Edgar Hoover might have had a few personal problems but his legacy in federal law enforcement is one of integrity and loyalty to the Constitution. His agents were and are still professional and hard-working.

Gregorio Santos had already been sentenced and was sitting in a maximum prison in Colorado for killing the Japanese jogger. It was relayed that Gregorio was taking his GED classes and had become religious. Carlos and Johnny were hoping that the latter was true. Many a convict takes up religion to get out of a cellblock, and to have cookies and milk after the evening services. It was also a chance to catch up on prison gossip and to see their "homies" from the streets.

Carlos and Tom Parker felt frustrated, not able to finish up some of their cases. The murders involving the Chinese couple were still a mystery, and the Thompsons were still missing. There was also the case of the two missing Filipino workers. There had been no trace of these women after they went back to their barracks. A check with the families back in the Philippines was fruitless, no contact of any kind, which was totally out of character for the young women. They were homebodies and faithful church goers.

There had been additional sightings of mysterious creatures and ghosts at both the Californian and Beach hotels, but it was usually during or after a long night of drinking or dope-smoking, or on a stormy night where the winds reached near-typhoon conditions or when some fool ran his car off the road and he blamed it on some witch who stepped out in front of him.

Both Carlos and Tom had seen mysterious objects in the sky, possibly missiles being fired or new experimental airplanes. As well, they had observed several "green flashes," an easily explained phenomenon that occurs as the sun sets over the horizon of the ocean, and the green portion of the color spectrum flashes across the sky for a few seconds. The weather has to be perfect for this to be seen—usually a cloudless sky.

Tom and Carlos were enjoying a leisurely breakfast and talking about beating the bushes, shake things up a bit, and have something/anything break lose on the open cases. Cocina joined them at breakfast, carrying the Guam newspaper.

She said, "I think you'll find page two interesting." There it was! The headline read, "Two people missing—Unknown Circumstances."

Carlos called up a detective buddy on Guam. The detective said that the couple, a Chinese man and a woman, had been missing for two days, and there were absolutely no leads.

Carlos asked, "Were they tourists?"

The detective answered, "We did a profile on them with the Chinese police. The Beijing Police said that they were known dealers; and to watch for more drug activity." Again, the officers said that their borders had been closed off and the dealers were trying different places to bring in dope.

Carlos inquired, "Did the Chinese check with the families?"

"Yes, they did. The families said that they hadn't heard from the couple, and that the man had borrowed the equivalent of four thousand dollars to send to their family members in San Francisco."

"Did you get all the info on our missing people?"

"Yeah, I have the notification bulletin in front of me. Seems to be the same MO."

The detective added, "Here's some info for you. Several members of Yakuza have been spotted at the beach hotels. Fits their style—they're going first class. We know it's them—I had one of my Japanese investigators drop by and take a gander. Three males covered with tattoos, and two of them were missing fingers."

Carlos stated, "That's all we need—the Japanese Mafia. They're bad ass dudes. I always picture them as 'Samurai Gone Bad.' They have definite codes of conduct and try to give off the image of Robin Hood. There's quite a magazine account about them helping the citizenry after the huge Japanese tsunami, which they did in the beginning but later on, they were questionably being given many of the lucrative contracts in rebuilding."

The detective added, "You wouldn't think the dope market would be big enough for them to dabble."

"You'd think so but they deal in everything from vice and gambling, and of course, drugs are lucrative with China shutting down the trade. A lot of ice is manufactured in Japan, so maybe it's a concerted move on their part. Our islands are small, but we get a lot of travelers. It would be a good transit point to America and Canada, or even to Europe. Also, many of our flights go to Australia and New Zealand."

"The Yakuza doesn't like competition so maybe that eliminating small-time dealers like the Chinese and the Americans."

"Or how about the manufacturers on Guam—make their own product?"

"Not now; we had a start-up factory but they managed to blow themselves up. Now there are federal laws in place that prohibit the needed chemicals from being imported. I suppose that will lead to more smuggling, but so far, Customs hasn't found anything like that yet."

Carlos concluded, "No factory on Saipan so far. Please keep us posted on whatever you discover. I'll let the FBI and DEA know at our end. Maybe we can roadblock the whole scheme in the beginning."

"Tough to do when the abusers want the dope. We'll never stop the supply with the giant demand. It's all about dopeheads and money."

"Sad, but true! In the meanwhile, a message has been sent to the underground operators."

Chapter 26

MUCHACHOS AND WAR STORIES

All cops have good stories to tell. They deal with real life and human frailties. They know the veracities of what happens in real incidents on the job, and have a difficult time watching "cop" shows on television and in the movies. Statistics and interviews have revealed that about only forty percent of TV viewers find fictional TV shows to be accurate in content, and only about fourteen percent of law enforcement officers see the cop shows as being correct. Most police officers do not watch police shows. When they deal with victims and criminals on the job, they can't stomach all the misinformation that is broadcasted out to the public through the television and movie episodes.

Sometimes this misinformation makes it difficult to work with the public on their own, very personal cases. Citizens expect DNA results to come back in less than an hour, and that barricaded suspects can be talked out in the same time-frame. Also, if a perp won't talk, the officer should put him under a bright, hot light and slap him around until he talks. On TV, citizens often see a knife-wielding criminal charging a policeman, and the bad guy is taken down with a ju-jitsu movement. In real life, a man with a knife can attack and make physical contact before the officer can draw his firearm from the holster. Knives are deadly. So the officer, like the Boy Scouts, always has to "be prepared," or the officer will be sentenced to a lavish funeral at an early age complete with bagpipes and grieving family and associates.

Cops working together for twenty to thirty years form a strong bond of camaraderie and understanding of each other and what happens on the job, and that holds true from jurisdiction to jurisdiction. A New York and an Oregon cop can fall into a natural conversation within minutes—there is a brotherhood/sisterhood of guys and gals who have been on the battleground of life and death for their entire careers. Things can change in fractions of seconds on the job, from eating a donut to the next moment of sheer terror.

When cops get together socially, many of their adventures often become the topics of conversation. All officers know "suicide by cop," where the suspect charges or threatens the cop, and the cop has to defend himself, and the cop takes out the suspect, now a victim of suicide. Cops all know that in all conversations, there will be stories about over-zealous cops, and more so if a civilian joins the group. Just like most criminals who are mostly innocent, the same holds true for traffic law offenders. They know accounts of stupid bank robbers who drop their wallets at the crime scene, or lock their keys in the get-away car or forget to fill up their gas tanks.

There is always humor on the job. There has to be because humor is a great releaser of stress and fright. There is always banter going back and forth.

Carlos had some great "language" stories, Saipan being a diverse part of humanity, Korean, Japanese, Chinese, Bangladeshi, and the local Filipino, Chamorro and Carolinians. One of his favorite was a traffic stop he made when he was in uniform. The car was driven by a local dope dealer and Carlos was hoping to catch the guy dirty. He asked for a driver's license which was scratched and hard to read. So he gave the man a ticket for "mutilated license." When he handed the ticket to the driver, the man asked, "Why did you give me this ticket?" He explained that the license was mutilated. The man replied, "That's *bula-bula*. My license doesn't expire for another eight months."

In a murder case, Carlos recalled the defendant's mother came up from Palau to influence the trial of her son. She stared continually at the jurors and the word was spread about that she was a witch. She was observed cracking open eggs and spreading chicken feathers in the restroom and dried materials on the benches in the courtroom.

She was spotted again sprinkling dried blood dust on hallway doors. It was described by her followers as a powerful voodoo powder. The judge went to his bench one morning and found a large sea shell and feathers on his chair. He then called her into his office and told her to stop with the witch doctor nonsense. Even with her special powers, the son was convicted by the jury in less than two hours. The mother wasn't disgraced because spectators later surmised that likely her magic powers were only effective on Palau.

In another incident, Carlos a got call to aid a woman at a local hot spot managed by a Chinese man. When he arrived, he asked the man waiting for him if he was the proprietor. The man replied in the negative and said that he was the owner. He took Carlos back to the woman, a Filipina, who was on the floor twitching. He asked the man if she was epileptic. The man replied, "I don't know for sure but I think she's a Catholic." Time after time, he ran into "Engrish" problems, especially when working vice. The Chinese prosties could carry on a conversation in a bar, set a price, which hotel, which position, etc., but once in court, the lady absolutely knew no English. Through an interpreter, the ladies invariably thought they were going "to a party" with free drinks, and that the man would give them $100 just for pocket money. The stock answer was like out of a street manual, similar to beating a DWI charge in court, "How to Beat the Vice Cop in Court."

One of Carlos' favorite stories was about a car swerving from side to side of the first lane along the Beach Road. He figured "drunk driver," but when he approached the car, he could see only a small white Maltese dog. The car was driven by a very small Asian woman. She was dwarfed by her large yacht-cruiser car. The dog was sitting on top of her head, and now became possessive and barked at the officer. The Asian woman said, "So sorry. While I'm driving, dog jump on head. He wouldn't get on seat." Carlos decided not to reach inside the car for a license and insurance card, and take a chance on being bitten to death by a five-pound dog. So he told the woman to put the dog on the car seat, and to pull over if the dog decided to sit on her head again. Cops think there will never be another story to top this one—but there will be.

After working over twenty years in Los Angeles, Tom Parker was loaded down with "war stories." Many of his stories are sad and tragic, but he had a few to keep the evening jovial. One dark evening, a lady was robbed in South-central LA and the officers nabbed the guy that matched the description. The officers took the suspect back in a field show-up to ask the lady if the caught suspect was the robber. The procedure isn't perfect because the suspect is in handcuffs in a police car, and there is always the concern that the victim will be convinced that was the guy who robbed her. They brought the lady to the suspect and as the police car pulled up, the suspect spontaneously said to an officer, "Yep, that's the one I robbed." Duh!

Tom also mentioned that there were plenty of wanna be actors and models on the California police and fire forces. He mentioned a handsome Hispanic guy nicknamed "Hollywood Guapo" who was a good cop; and he moonlighted as a successful model and was often spotted on billboards and clothing catalogs. The guys liked to rag on him—he was always combing back his black hair and applying face cream before and after work.

One day an old timer, Roberto, happened to walk by and he said, "Damn, you're pretty. I think probably you look spend more time in the mirror than my wife." Guapo replied, "That's because I'm better looking than your wife." You could have heard a pin drop in the locker room Roberto took it well. His response was simply, "You may be right. You're one gorgeous cop." Kidding back and forth was common and done good-naturedly.

FBI Agent Dan Simpson dropped by—the smell of Guangman's fresh-baked cinnamon rolls must travel several miles to FBI Headquarters. Dan joined right in and had his share of federal stories, like when the "coyotes" dug up a tunnel that led from Mexico to Arizona to transport drugs and to bring in illegal immigrants. The tunnel exited into a large warehouse. The Border Patrol notified Immigration Officers and rather than shutting down the tunnel, together they pulled in non-descript buses and paddy wagons outside the warehouse for transportation of prisoners. Before the day was over, they had managed to arrest over a hundred for illegal entry, six more for illegal drugs, and five of the coyotes. The warehouse was demolished by court order and the tunnel filled in with heavy rocks.

Another federal story was the one about the Italian tomato grower. He was getting too old and decrepit to till the soil, and the soil was turning to clay after the spring rains. His sons said that they were too busy with their jobs and families to come help. The oldest son said, "Don't worry, Dad. I've got an idea." Two days later, three DEA agents showed with back hoes and a work crew of ten men. They held the old man off to the side as they went about their business of digging up the yard, and flipping the soil back and forth. They just told the old man they were looking for loot from a bank job. They didn't find anything and smoothed out the soil so that it was level. The old man called his son and asked "What the hell happened with those federal guys." The son answered, "I pretended to be a confidential informant. I told them that you were an old, retired wise guy and these were money and drugs buried in your yard." The old man planted his tomatoes two days later.

Going back in history, Dan talked about his beloved FBI, originally organized in 1908 as the Bureau of Investigation; but because of all the gangster activity, Hoover was brought aboard and in 1935, the FBI took on its current designation. Dan mentioned that Al Capone was the first person to make the FBI's Most Wanted List. During their early days, the term "racketeering" was coined in 1927. In 1934, the FBI, coordinating with local police, managed to shoot down these public enemies: Bonnie and Clyde, John Dillinger, Pretty Boy Floyd, and Baby Face Nelson. The first FBI agent to be killed in the line of duty was Edwin Shanahan in 1925. Dan said that the FBI had been involved with gang warfare from the time of Prohibition onward. One of his training officers had been around in the 1950's when Joseph "Crazy Joey" Gallo was gunned down for at Umberto's Clam House in New York City for supposedly ordering the hit on mobster Joe Colombo. The assassination occurred on Crazy Joey's 43rd birthday, and of all people, Don Rickles was performing. Again with the dark humor, agents were saying "Betcha Don got out of town fast after this one," and "It takes on a whole new meaning when your act kills the audience." By the way, Dan mentioned that crime has never been solved.

Carlos said, "We might be needing your federal forces to help stop the Japanese Mafia, the Yakuza. The local cops won't have a clue on how to deal with their organization and tactics. We've had some information that they have been seen on Guam. We don't know much about them, except they can be deadly."

Dan shifted his large frame in his chair as he reached for another cinnamon roll and stated, "You mean those fictional characters that do karate with Jackie Chan and Chuck Norris in the movies?"

"Yep, that be the ones. They've been described as wearing black suits, most tattoos covered up, donning expensive sun glasses, and missing fingers. The Guam officers stated that they walk about as 'the cock on the walk.' Every body always clears a path as they stroll anymore, including the beach and dining rooms. You can tell that the Asians fear, or maybe respect, them."

Dan said, "They're bad asses. They have a sort of "Robin Hood" persona with the people but they commit loathsome criminal acts. They don't operate much in the USA, except for the occasional killing and then vanish back to Japan. Maybe the worldwide down shift in the economy is making them realize they need to expand their interests, even to something legitimate."

Carlos asked, "Details? We need info to offset these guys, to get their butts back into Asia."

"Chances are they have something to do with our missing people."

Carlos said, "Would be good to find out."

Dan answered, "This is what I know about these criminals. We've had numerous trainings and working with Homeland Security."

Chapter 27

THE JAPANESE YAKUZA

FBI Agent Dan Simpson related what he knew about the Yakuza, a well-known criminal syndicate in Japan with its lawless tentacles reaching throughout the world in various ways. And now possibly they were coming to Guam and Saipan.

Dan explained: "Dating back to the 1600's, it is historically told that they allegedly stole from the rich and gave to the poor. Their history indicates that they came from *machi-yokko* (servants of the town) who protected the villages from rogue samurai. It is also related that the original Yakuza were the criminal samurai—so who's to believe? Whether they began as heroes or villains, the Yakuza are proud to be outcasts from the normal levels of society—a fact reflected in the name: ya means 8, *ku* means 9, and *sa* means 3, which adds up to 20—a losing hand in the card game *hana-fuda* (flower cards). Translated, it means the Yakuza are the "bad hands" or "losers" of society," an image they embrace."

They reminded Carlos of the American "Hell's Angels," another group paradoxically feared and respected, and always exciting. People love to hear the roar of their Harleys but they definitely do not want the ragtag mavericks near their daughters.

"The Yakuza is not a single entity but rather a collection of gangs, much like the Mafia, but with a more intricate hierarchy. Within the crime syndicate are several "powerful" families; the *ichi bon* is the Yamaguchi-Gumi family, with about 45,000 members. In all, it is estimated there are 2,500 families and more than 100,000 Yakuza, making it the largest criminal organization in the world. The Mexican and Latin cartels are huge and powerful but not united, and are constantly battling one another. They do as much damage to each another, as the Mexican army and police combined together.

"The activity is spread out from Japan to Hawaii and beyond. They own casinos in Las Vegas, operate construction companies in Chicago and London, and produce movies in Hollywood and Hong Kong. Each family is made of up of many sub-gangs or clans. At the head of each family group is a *kumicho*, a godfather figure. There are several other sub-groups of leadership, all the way to *oyabun*, who are the clan bosses. They each have a group of trusted men, who act as the local bosses, and so on down to the bottom level, *kobun* (the youngsters and newbies). Once accepted, each kobun is assigned to an oyabun. The elder members instructs and watches over his apprentice, and is responsible for the youngster's action. The members consider this relationship to be more sacred than that of father and son.

"Just like inner city gangs in the USA, kids are drawn to the gangs with the fancy cars and tons of yen. The money can be quite good. Yakuza families earn about sixty billion dollars annually, nearly 2% of Japan's GNP; but it will take years for new recruits to start seeing any big dividends. Any money they make must be turned over to their oyabuns. Harmony within the groups is also paramount to keeping order, requiring a few basic tenets: Never reveal any secrets of the organization, never harm wives and children; don't use drugs; don't withhold money from the gang; always obey your superior, and don't ask the police for help. Above all else, loyalty to the family is the glue that holds the Yakuza together.

"Besides the risks being involved in crime, there are other dangers involved such as hepatitis. The tattoos tell the story and history of the member. Japanese tattoo artists use a technique called *tebori*—attaching a small bundle of needles to a bamboo handle, which is dipped in ink and tapped into the skin by hand or with a small hammer. This method is notorious for spreading infections. In addition, the ink inhibits the sweating out of toxins. These issues combined with heavy drinking, leads to a high incidence of liver damage among the membership. The tattooing process can cost up to $10,000 plus years of painful pinpricks to endure.

"If an obun angers or causes embarrassment to his oyabun, he is obligated to cut off the tip of his pinkie finger and present to his boss gift-wrapped. A second offense calls for the severing of the second joint of that finger, and so on. This punishment, called *yubizume*, comes from the traditional way of holding Japanese holding a sword—removing the pinkie and ring fingers progressively weakens a warrior's grip. A family member knows that he must commit yubizume when his superior gives him a knife and a piece of string—the knife to cut off the finger and the string to stop the bleeding. Serious offenses require a suicide *seppuku*—ritual disembowelment with a sword.

Becoming a Yakuza member is as easy as walking into one of their offices and filling out an application. Because it is not illegal to be a member, they're quite open about their existence. Each office has a wooden sign out front that displays the name of the family. Members carry business cards. Some publish their own magazines, advertise, march in parades and even send recruiters to schools and prisons. There are no specific requirements to join up—except one. You must be male. The only woman recognized in a Yakuza family is the boss's wife, the *ane-san*, which means 'little sister.' Though she does not participate in criminal activity, all members must show her the same respect they show the boss. This gender part is significant in police investigations because there is no known caper where a female was an undercover agent or an integral part of the actual criminal enterprise."

Carlos said, "It's easy to see how they recruit youngsters into their organization. The members are like kings in their neighborhood, get a lot of respect, and drive those fancy cars. With money and power, the ladies are attracted to the members like moths to light, and bees to honey. The young men see the females as another bonus for sure."

Horoto had joined the group, and added, "The Yakuza are powerful people in Japan. They always play up an image as champions of the down-trodden and the outcasts, providing havens for *burakumin* (a segregated group of 'untouchables'). They also provide a home for high school dropouts, kids that can't keep up with the highly competitive school system. They also adopt the rougher elements of society and end up disciplining and taming these wild kids and help to minimize violent acts against ordinary people."

Dan added, "It is often thought that the Yakuza has helped to keep Japan's crime rate at one of the lowest in the world. These kids then adapt to the traditional way of operating. They get into extortion, money laundering, some gun running and narcotics sales and prostitution. Like any pyramid scheme, those at the top make the most money. One way to go up the rung is building your own gang until you become a local boss. The gangs don't hesitate to extort CEO's and other successful people about known mistresses; or doing something as subtle as printing a good review about a play or musical to boost sales. They dabble in just about anything to make money but avoid alarming the police and their local communities.

"Generally the relationships between Japanese authorities and the Yakuza are complex. Some of the police admire the Yakuza's code of chivalry. As long as the gangsters are not too disruptive, the police mostly leave them alone. In return, the mobsters occasionally turn in a member of a gang to help the cops "solve" a case. It's the same with society as well. Society comes to appreciate the harmony in a neighborhood created by the Yakuza's presence. For example, after a car accident, instead of hiring lawyers, one party might hire a Yakuza member called a *jiken-ya* to propose a settlement. Generally the settlement is fair and made without threats or violence.

Horoto said, "Dan-san, I believe you know more about the Yakuza than I do. They are usually in the shadows, and the general populations know very little about them, or even see them. When they do show up, it's usually about a good deed, like making a contribution to a children's park or helping out an old destitute widow."

Dan asked, "You're Japanese. How do you feel about them?"

"Back home, the first thing I would consider was to be to be careful about what I was saying, and not to anger the Yakuza family. I've never crossed them or felt their wrath. Others have, judging by the bodies that occasionally surface in Tokyo Bay."

Dan said, "A lot of things are changing within the ranks of Yakuza. Many of the families are going legit and avoiding all violence. Japan is a society of rigid rules and traditions and the Yakuza break many of them. They remain outcasts, even with their millions of dollars. Tattoos and missing fingers are strictly taboo among the Japanese citizenry, and those that flaunt them are often shunned. But there is still a wild, lawless element within the organization, and they may be the younger ones that are intending to break away from their elders. They could be the ones trying to make a name for themselves in virgin territories like Guam and Saipan."

Carlos declared, "We'll do everything we can to stop it. The Guam Police are on board professionally, and have been doing some training classes. They have already contracted with three Japanese-American translators. Time will tell the story on this one."

Dan agreed, "Also, the federal agencies are primed and ready . . . that's why we've been doing the training. Intelligence sources tell us that the Yakuza is getting more aggressive. The agents back in LA are waiting to see the clash between the Yakuza and the real Italiano Mafia."

Carlos laughed and said, "Now, that will make a great movie!"

Chapter 28

ANNA AND MARIE— THE MISSING FILIPINAS

Life was quasi-normal on Saipan. The big news, meaning more hotel occupancy and restaurant patronage, was that the US Immigration authorities' finally allowed Chinese and Russia tourists to come to Saipan on a visitor's visa. One beautiful tropical day was followed by another—each day seemed to blend into the next. It was a very predictable existence except for the occasional crooked politician heading for a federal prison or some stupid killing by machete over a girlfriend. There should have been more going to the hoosegow but the FBI and Federal Prosecutors were overloaded. As for sending out more help from Washington, D.C., there was plenty of work to be done on the Mainland with illegal immigration, gun-running and racketeering.

Economic times were tough on Saipan. The economy was worse than ever because tourism was generally down and the unemployment rate escalated to over thirty percent. People were searching for ways of making a living. Women that had never considered prostitution as a career choice were now turning tricks in Garapan or home delivery with special massage services. Young men were stealing, not just for food and fuel, but also for their drugs and to play poker.

These situations gave Carlos, Johnny, Horoto, Tom and Dan their first big break in the missing Filipinas, Anna and Marie, the two new housekeepers at the Californian Hotel. And it happened because of money—somebody needed money over loyalty to one friends and family. Crimestoppers took the anonymous call. The organization's motto is "Fight crime without revealing your identity," and they mean it.

Crimestoppers has gone international and has been extremely successful, especially in the United States. Since its inception in Albuquerque, New Mexico in 1975, Crimestoppers has been responsible for over a half-million arrests and the recovery of over four billion dollars in stolen goods and money. Fear and apathy often are two of the poisonous ingredients that stop witnesses and those that have knowledge from calling the police. Crimestoppers is a charitable corporation and protects the caller from being identified, and if the information is correct a cash reward is given.

The president of the local branch of Crimestoppers, Jesse Collins, came by the Beach Hotel and offered possible clues about two possible suspects in the mysterious disappearance of the two Filipinas. Jesse said, "I believe this is good information. The informant called in from an unidentifiable number, and spoke to my volunteer at the call center. Basically, the caller said that the two women were cut up by a machete and buried in different parts of the Marpi mountain areas. The caller said that the two local men were waiting near the barracks in a large white van. When the women appeared, the suspects exited the van and applied handcuffs and blind folds on the girls."

Carlos stated, "That's a lot of info so far. What else?"

The caller said that he is related to the suspects by marriage and didn't like what they did. He said that the men started bragging about the women at fiestas. One night, they were drunk and got into a fight with three other guys. He said that they got beat up pretty badly and drank some more cheap rum for pain, and then by daybreak they were babbling how they killed the women. First, they said they raped them repeatedly, and then tied them and locked them up in a deserted barn. Later in the day, they came back and molested the women again. They had decided to kill and dismember the women. They had brought their sharp machetes."

Carlos asked, "Did the caller give any names?"

Jesse continued, "That's the best part. He gave the names, Juan Guerrero and John Baker. They're cousins also. He knows where they live and they still have the white van. The van plate is EGW117."

Tom Parker asked, "Did you give this info to the police?"

Jesse answered, "Of course. But they'll likely have a tough time getting off their butts and out of the air-conditioned office. Besides, I think Guerrero is related to several of the cops."

Carlos said, "Much appreciated. Got time for a quick lunch, some Korean specialties?"

Jesse replied, "Love to but I have to get to my real job—the one that pays the bills. This volunteer stuff makes you feel good but doesn't pay for the utilities."

Tom said, "We appreciate the info. We'll let you know if we come up with anything.

Horoto asked, "If the caller is anonymous, how do you make the payoff for good information?"

Jesse said, "The caller is assigned a number, no names, and then when the info works out, we arrange a drop site—could be under a large rock in San José or buried under the sand at Wing Beach in front of the last picnic table. We don't monitor the pickup by the caller."

The men shook hands and Carlos, Tom and Dan reconvened at the smaller, private table. The others went to work.

Dan said, "I can claim jurisdiction because the victims are from another country, which therefore makes it an international incident."

Carlos added, "We need to get the van and soon. Even though time has passed, there might still be info inside. I've known suspects that kept souvenir clothing, like panties and bras, for months after the crime. Also we need to find out if these guys have girlfriends. Some of the hotel Filipinas said that the victims had gold rings and necklaces. Crooks can't stop themselves from trying to impress their squeezes with gifts."

Dan asserted, "I'm going to write up an affidavit on what we have so far, then get an impound on the van."

"While the van is being impounded, Carlos and I will pay a simultaneous visit to John Baker. He's not related to any of the players. He might be willing to blame everything on Guerrero," said Tom.

Meanwhile, Carlos and Tom had done a drive-by in the neighborhood and confirmed the license plate number of the van. It was registered to Guerrero. They also noticed that John Baker kept irregular hours, sometimes drinking all day and other times heading for the poker palace. Two days later at daybreak, Dan made his move with a court order and sent over a tow truck for the van. As luck would have it, Baker was still in bed. He came out when he heard the van being towed. Guerrero wasn't at the location.

Tom and Carlos introduced themselves. They told Baker right up front they were there to talk about the missing Filipinas. Baker's face tightened and he turned beet red, definitely signs of a guilty man with a conscience. He couldn't hold eye contact. He asked, "What are you guys doing with Juan's truck. He let me use it last night, and he's going to be pissed when he knows it's been towed."

Tom decided to be direct and said, "That's the least of your worries, Amigo. Tell us about the two girls that you murdered." Tom and Carlos were both civilians and need not advise Baker of his Constitutional rights.

Baker said, "You guys aren't shit. I don't have to talk to you."

Carlos answered, "That's true. We'll send the FBI agents over to you. They're ready to put you in the federal pen for life."

"Okay, let me think about it. Maybe we can cut a deal. It wasn't me that killed the girls. It was that crazy Juan. He said we had to get rid of the girls so they couldn't talk."

With Baker in front, Tom and Carlos meandered over to a picnic table under a giant mango tree, and heard Baker confess to helping and being at the murders. He said that he helped kidnap the girls and had sex with them at the deserted barn. He said that he had no idea that Juan intended to kill them later. The men had sex with the girls again. He added that the girls were cooperative because they thought they were going to be freed up. They even promised not to tell anyone about the rape."

Carlos inquired, "Then what happened?"

Baker continued, "Suddenly, Juan pulled out a large Bowie knife and stabbed them to death. They died instantly. He then went to the van and pulled out his machete, and started to cut them into pieces. He said that we didn't need witnesses and if we took the pieces of the girls to different places, the feral cats and dogs would eat them up. Maybe that's what happened. We put the body parts in the van, and then he dropped me at my house. I haven't heard any more about the deaths, until you guys showed up."

"What else? Did you help transport the body parts in the van? To a grave site?"

"I helped put the body parts in large garbage bags but I didn't go to any grave sites." Baker whimpered, "I'm glad you guys came. This situation had been driving me loco for months on end—I can barely sleep."

Tom's facial expression displayed no sign of sympathy and he asked, "Tell us about Juan. Does he have guns?"

"Yeah, he's got a .38 Smith and Wesson pistol, and a shotgun and rifle. He knows how to use them. We've done target practice a lot of times."

Tom and Carlos relayed the information to Agent Dan Simpson, who promptly took Baker into custody. Carlos told Dan to watch for a knife and machete, and blood stains, in the truck when the FBI did the processing of the van. They also warned Dan about Juan's guns.

Carlos later asked, smiling, "Feel sorry for the little creep?"

"Yeah. I am so sorry that he can't sleep. What's with these unfeeling AH's?"

"Who knows? Two young women gone . . . no marriages and babies, and a life full of happiness in front of them . . . all erased . . . and now they're on the long sleep." He added, "Freaking psychopaths aren't motivated by love or fear or rage or hatred. They don't feel emotion."

Tom said, "Let's help Dan get that other goon."

"Drive on."

Chapter 29

ROUNDING UP KILLER JUAN

Somebody must have tipped Juan Guerrero that the FBI was looking for him. He was no where to be found. The FBI had kept Baker away from a jail telephone for several hours but one of Juan's relatives in the jail probably let him know that he should start hiding. Likely also those law enforcement relatives knew that Juan was a killer and chose to do nothing about it, forgetting their law enforcement oath. Dan had already closed off the airports and seaport and had an informant watching the Smiling Cove Marina for someone matching Juan's description renting or stealing a boat. The closest place to sail would be Guam, but those authorities and the Coast Guard were alerted also.

Before he was jailed, Baker told Carlos and Tom that the victims had been wearing gold chains and rings, and that Juan had taken them off their bodies before they were hacked up. He also said that Juan considered himself quite "the lover boy" and had three girlfriends in town. He said that they were initially girlfriends, but after Juan dated them once or twice, they dumped him faster than they could spit. But one girl had gone with him several times, Laurie Gomez, and Juan bragged that he had given her the jewelry and she opened up her whole body to him.

Baker figured it was a lie but Tom and Carlos decided to check it out. They found her at the local college. They saw that she wearing a gold necklace and had a gold bracelet on each wrist. Carlos explained why they were talking to her. She immediately took off the gold and gave it to

Carlos. She lamented, "I should have known better than take anything from that jerk. He said his old auntie had left the gold to him. While I was wearing the gold, I just pretended that someone else had given the jewelry to me . . . but I feel so disgusted now that I am wearing those poor girls' jewelry." She started to cry. She added, "I should never have gone out with him the second time. He had already given me the gold and right afterwards, he tried to unsnap my bra. What a low life."

Tom asked, "Know where we can find him? We're trying to help the FBI on this case. Does he have a cell phone?

"I'm not sure where he lives. His cell phone doesn't have a load—I think he just carries it around for appearances."

Carlos said, "I know where a lot of the Guererros live. They might give us some help." Carlos and Tom were packing semi-auto Glocks with fifty extra rounds.

Tom and Carlos arrived in the As Lito village, and found some of the older people sitting in the shade under an orchid tree. They were drinking ice tea. Carlos explained what was happening with Juan. Tom noticed Carlos always got a lot of respect from most people they talked to—he had a sterling reputation. A lot of the people suggested that he go back on the police force or run for a political office. Carlos always deferred saying that he liked the hotel business and regular hours.

One of the older gents, Francisco Guererro, became the spokesman for the group. He was Juan's uncle and obviously a traditional leader. He advised that everyone knew that Juan was running from the FBI and that he was wanted for murder. The word was out. The old coconut express, drums and gossip, was every bit as effective as television announcements.

They had checked his room, and his guns were gone. Francisco promised cooperation and that if they heard from him, they would talk him into surrendering. He realized that he would be no match for FBI sharpshooters with high-powered rifles. Tom asked, "How did you know a Special Weapons Team was coming over from Guam?"

Francisco looked at Carlos and smiled, "The old ways are still good ways. We knew within a few hours of the telephone call to Guam. The Team should be here in about two hours."

Tom asked, "Maybe you can help us find him and talk him into coming with us? We promise not to hurt him and we'll get him safe passage to the jailhouse."

Francisco said, "My young nephews have already talked to him. They know the cave on the mountain where he hides. It is a great hiding place—the Japanese used it after World War II but finally surrendered when they needed food and medical supplies."

"He won't come down?"

"He told my nephews that he would never surrender. He can't imagine spending his whole life in jail." Carlos thought to himself, "Jail is too good for this gruesome piece of garbage. He needs to have a taste of his own medicine—a rusty dull machete came to mind."

Tom asked, "Can we go talk to him?"

Francisco replied, "Okay by me. I'll send one of my nephews ahead. He will talk to you in the river-bed cleared area below the cave."

"How about an ambush?"

The old man, "He won't. It is a family honor situation. I told him not to act stupid or sneaky."

"My nephew Charles will guide you. It will take you about an hour to get to the clearing." He handed Tom and Carlos a water canteen. He said, "You'll need this. And keep your guns holstered so he doesn't feel threatened."

Carlos notified the FBI and Johnny that they were heading up the mountain to meet with Juan. Dan was worried about their safety but Carlos convinced him that a small party might be able to coax him down the hill. He said that if he didn't come down voluntarily, that it could take months to have him come down. Carlos reminded Dan that it took six months to talk Captain Oba of the Japanese Imperial Army off the mountain to surrender, and Oba had to worry about his soldiers, as well as taking care of women and children.

Tom and Carlos started up the mountain with Charles in the lead. The jungle was thick and dense, but Charles knew the tails and openings. It began raining in torrents, and the sky lit up with lightning. Charles yelled, "The Gods bring the thunda." During several of the thunder blasts, the ground shook and the trees bent low. It was scary and invigorating at the same time. They were drenched.

The loud storm broke and moved away in thirty minutes. After an hour, Charles said, "Juan will be under the copse of trees just ahead."

Tom and Carlos sensed that the trees would be a good ambush spot. They knew Juan had a rifle for long distance, and a shotgun for up close. Remembering their Marine days ('never bunch up'), they separated and moved slowly towards the trees. Charles yelled out for Juan to show himself.

Suddenly a flock of birds took to the sky. The jungle became quiet—eerie and surreal. The sun reflected off the huge green leaves.

Juan stepped from behind a large rock and told Carlos and Tom to drop their pistols to the ground. Both Carlos and Tom knew that it couldn't and wouldn't happen. They had worked together before and knew that disarming themselves would lead to instant death. Juan did not have a weapon in his hands but had a handgun in his waistband and a rifle slung over his shoulders with a leather sling.

Carlos yelled back, "We'll keep our pistols holstered, now step out so we can see you."

They walked within twenty yards of each other. Carlos told Juan why they were there and they would escort him so he could safely surrender and be booked into the jail.

Tom watched his eyes and body language. All his experience and instincts had taught him that Juan wasn't going to surrender. While Carlos did the talking, Tom did the watching.

Juan was fidgeting and fumbling over his words.

He then yelled out, "There's no sense in me giving up. They'll send me away for life. I hate the idea of living in a concrete box." He slouched to the left side and drew the handgun from his waistband. As he moved, Tom was already focused on him and had his hand on his Glock. Tom knew if Juan raised his gun, he would have to take him out.

Juan raised his gun and pointed it at Carlos. Tom drew and fired two quick shots hitting Juan full-chest. As he dropped, he managed to fire off one round into the dirt. Carlos ran forward and threw a set of handcuffs on Juan. He kicked Juan's gun off to the side.

"Another suicide by cop! He didn't have the guts to kill himself," said Carlos.

Charles didn't make a move, nor did the other cousin, Reynaldo, who was watching from a higher pile of rocks. Carlos was watching their hands.

Carlos checked Juan for a pulse. There was none. The bleeding was minimal; the heart had absorbed both bullets and the man was dead.

"We got the bastard before he could hit us." He added, "He meant what he said—no surrender."

The two cousins had come down and saw the body. Surprisingly, Charles said, "No loss. He was a bad man."

Carlos asked, "Did he commit other crimes?"

Charles summarized, "He was always doing something stupid or hurtful. He drove his family crazy with worries, and we all endured many days of embarrassment. He was a mean bully. He even raped one of our girl cousins."

Carlos called the FBI and arranged for a body pickup by helicopter in a nearby field. After the chopper arrived, Dan alighted and took photos for later explanation of the shooting. He took witness statements from Charles and Reynaldo. Both cousins agreed that Juan had drawn first and that Tom was defending himself, as well as protecting Carlos and the cousins.

Tom and Carlos decided to walk out and explain everything to Francisco Guerrero.

As the chopper lifted off, Carlos whispered to the wind, "May God have mercy on his rotten soul."

Tom said, "Now, we need to find the victims so they can have a proper burial or their remains returned to their families in the Philippines."

Charles overheard them. He said, "I think I know where the girls are buried."

After trekking back to the Guererro compound, they rested; and then struck out again with family members and shovels. The victims were buried in a grave of mixed body parts in gray garbage bags, not over 300 yards from the compound. Juan had lied to his accomplice Baker when he said he would spread all the parts over various sections of the island.

Of course, to the end, Juan was a liar, and too lazy to dig more graves.

The Medical Examiner arrived and took over the grim recovery.

DNA results from the FBI lab revealed they were in fact the two missing Filipina women. There were also traces of their blood in the white van. A machete was recovered in the van, as well as a large knife—both had blood residue in the crevasses of the handles. There were complete matchups. Carlos thought, "We always catch the dumb ones."

John Baker pled guilty to second degree murder, kidnapping and rape. For his "cooperation," he was sentenced to thirty years in prison. Not enough!

Chapter 30

ANOTHER JOGGER FOUND

All the missing people had been accounted for except the Thompsons and the missing Russian jogger near the Duty Free Shops. She had been jogging in broad daylight, and there were no reports or witnesses to her abduction. After this crime, and the horrendous treatment of several Russian tourist victims, Russia was warning its citizens about vacationing on Saipan. Security and safety are of paramount importance to all travelers. A safety alert had already been posted in Japan.

Carlos set his mind to solving this case. Along with Tom, they checked in with all their informants and went over carefully the reports from Crimestoppers. Nothing developed. They took Zeus and some his "sniffer" canine pals out to areas where bodies had been dumped before. There are usually roads to "dump areas" so the suspect can take his cargo to a remote spot, either dump or bury the victim, and be on his way in a few short minutes. These are remote areas without lights or residents, and seldom would anyone be out in these isolated areas except for lovers or people smoking dope, or murderers deposing of their victims.

One of the dog handlers from Hawaii came to Saipan on vacation and he brought his bloodhound along for additional searching and sniffing. Carlos laughed when the handler said there would be a fee, "Ten pounds of kibble and a daily swim in the lagoon."

Carlos promised at least twenty pounds of kibble for the dog, and daily cinnamon rolls and Korean coffee for the handler. The handler stayed two weeks with his dog and still no luck. During the stay, Carlos' favorite line each day at breakfast was, "If we didn't have bad luck, we wouldn't have any luck at all."

The handler was optimistic, "Something will break loose. It always does."

Meanwhile five husky Japanese men had been spotted at the Fiesta Hotel. They were wearing bright Aloha shirts and expensive sporty sunglasses. At the pool, it was obvious that their bodies were covered with tattoos and they were missing pinky fingers. The hotel informants said they brought in different Chinese girls every night and also drank heavily. They liked expensive whiskey. They were basically quiet and followed the hotel rules. There was no evidence of drugs, except smoking a little weed by the younger ones.

A few days later, Carlos and Johnny took Zeus and a few other mutts of questionable lineage, a menagerie of multi-colored dogs and different sizes, up a road to the old radar station. The dogs went about their jobs of sniffing and digging. Zeus had wandered off and was soon heard barking excitedly about a hundred yards away. Carlos exclaimed, "Zeus has probably found a shrew and is trying to dig the little critter out of its hole." Then all the dogs ran to Alpha-dog Zeus and were all soon barking and jumping around in anticipation of finding food.

When Carlos and Johnny joined the dogs, they noticed right away that there a human leg showing above the dirt. Carlos shooed away the dogs, and started digging with a broken tree branch. Another leg soon appeared.

Carlos said, "Johnny, please give Dan and the ME a call. I do believe we have found another buried body."

Carlos started snapping pictures of the area, and the exposed body. He stopped digging, waiting for the FBI to show up with their evidence gear and professional cameras.

As Dan was driving up, so was Police Lt. Felix Cabrera. As the lieutenant maneuvered his obese frame out of the patrol car, there was no greeting to Carlos except, 'What are you doing here, Old Man? Are you still trying to play cop, trying to remember your so-called glory days?"

Carlos replied, "Nice to see you, too."

Carlos turned to Dan and started to give him the details of finding the corpse. The dumbshit lieutenant took Carlos by the shoulder to turn him around, "Hey, I'm talking to you."

The answer was swift and sure. Zeus appeared from nowhere and stood growling at the lieutenant's feet, all one hundred pounds of upset Dobie.

Carlos smiled and said, "You talking to me?"

"Yeah, you. Call off your dog or I'll shoot him."

"First of all, before you could draw, he would have you by the throat. One heavy crunch from those jaws and you would be dead. And secondly, I'll tell you right up front, if you shot my dog, you'd catch a slug right between your eyes. I wouldn't hesitate to protect Zeus—he's been taking care of me for years. Whatever the scenario, you would be dead." He added, "So play nice, you got it?"

The lieutenant called over to the FBI man, Dan, and asserted, "You are a witness to this. This bozo threatened to shoot me, and he won't call off his dog."

Dan replied, "No problems until you got here. I've got work to do. Just go back to your donut shop or run over and cry on the governor's desk or kiss his ass."

Zeus let him back off. As the lieutenant got in his car, he yelled out the window, "You guys will be hearing from me. I'm going to get a warrant and arrest you for interfering with a crime investigation." As he left, he peeled his wheels like some impetuous teenager.

Carlos said, "Sounds like a good traffic violation to me, plus tearing up the government cars."

Dan said, "Ignore him. He's pipsqueak—probably never even got his GED. I'm getting real tired of his crap. If he keeps messing with the investigations, I'll take him down for lying to a federal officer. It's a good felony and would keep him in the hoosegow for several days."

Carlos kept the dogs back while the ME and Dan went about excavating the grave, and preserving every shred of evidence. The corpse was a female wearing only a blouse. She had a butterfly tattoo on her right thigh. There was dried caked residue on her thighs and face. For whatever reason, the insects had passed consuming this dried liquid on her body. Her skull has been bashed by a large blunt object.

The Russian jogger's family had already forwarded by DHL the genetic makeup and the dental records of the deceased. It was a quick matchup on the teeth, especially after several of the dentists confirmed that the dental charts matched the victim's teeth perfectly. DNA analysis took several days longer, using body fluids and the humorous and femur bones from the body—the confirmation was there. The family DNA match was accurate. The missing jogger was Nadena Romanoff of Moscow, Russia. The family wasn't aware of the tattoo.

Nadena could now be returned to her native Russia for a decent burial and a proper ceremony of remembrance and respect. Johnny and Tom sent letters of regret and condolences from their hotels to Nadena's parents regarding her terrible death. The parents heard nothing from the Saipan government or any of the tourist agencies.

Now, to find the knuckle-dragging miscreant. Carlos immediately put the word out to his informants and a $5000 reward was made available from the family. Money doesn't necessarily buy happiness but it will bring the scavengers out of the dark.

Chapter 31

TYPHOON GERTUDE

"Batten down the Hatches" took on a whole new meaning for Johnny and the hotel staff. Johnny had watched a "zillion" World War II and Korean war movies with his father, and every time, especially at sea, the first mate seemed to yell out the order to secure and lock down. Johnny learned that a typhoon was heading up from the equator to Saipan (15 degrees north). The typhoon had already caused extensive rain and wind damage to Kosrae and Pohnpei. It was now sitting on top of Chuuk and swirling about, taking huts and people off into eternity. FEMA and the Red Cross were already planning an emergency response but couldn't move in the direction of the major storm until it moved northwest.

Johnny and Tom Parker, and other hotel owners were busily putting up storm shutters and locking down anything that could blow away. Windows and sliding glass doors were criss-crossed up with duct tape. Fortunately, the work crews had experienced typhoons before and knew what had to be done. Johnny saw one of his maintenance guys cutting all the coconuts off the trees and placing them in locked concrete building. Johnny asked Carlos, "Why do have cut down all the coconuts? The trees will take months to grow the nuts back before they can be used for cooking. And besides, the guests are surprised and delighted to see coconuts actually growing on a tree and not magically appearing in a market produce section."

Carlos said, "Coconuts become flying projectiles, especially when the winds reach one hundred MPH. Some of those nuts weight five pounds, and you can imagine the damage they would do if they hit you alongside the head. They bang up cars and trucks all the time, and smash out windshields. But that stuff can be repaired, but not so easy for a brain concussion."

While taking a break, Johnny asked Horoto, "I hear a lot of these typhoons hit Japan . . . also China and the Philippines."

Horoto said, "The typhoons followed a natural westerly pattern from the southeast of the Pacific, and fly over our local Micronesian islands. There are seventeen countries associated with Asia that plan and work together, especially tracking the typhoon. Other parts of the world call the giant winds "hurricanes," but because the influence of the Asian countries, and the Greek world word *typhein* (to smoke), they have became known as "typhoons" in the West Pacific. Names for the typhoons come from these countries, from rotating lists, and usually the names refer to flowers, animals and astrological signs. Sometimes they named after people, and this year it happens to be Gertrude."

Johnny said, "I know didly-squat about typhoons. How do they develop?"

Horoto laughed, "I like some of your funny words. We studied typhoons in school and also in hotel preparation classes. There has to be certain ingredients for the typhoon to develop: warm sea surface temperatures, atmospheric instability, high humidity, a low pressure center, pre-existing low-level disturbances and a low vertical wind shear. All the conditions start a swirling action and the disturbances move across the sea, many times gaining speed and often unpredictable in its direction of travel. Typhoon season is highest between June and November, and the Pacific Ocean is noted for having the most typhoons and the most intense. Weathermen love to study in the Pacific regions."

Johnny asked, "How do we classify the differences between heavy rains and typhoons? I swear some of these torrential downpours are typhoons—it rains so hard you can't see your hand right in front of you."

"The scientists have come up with these classifications. Up to 38 MPH is considered a tropical depression, but once the winds reach 48 MPH, then it is called a tropical storm. We get a lot of those right here on Saipan. Once the winds reach 74 MPH, then it's a typhoon, and it is considered a super typhoon when the winds are up to 120 MPH. The winds are measured with special instruments for one minute durations."

Johnny wanted to know, "Has Saipan been hit so hard that people are killed?"

"Typhoon Kim landed on the island a few years back. It knocked the hell out of everything for months—power, roads, telephones, and so on. A few people have been killed and injured in the typhoons here but usually because they are out driving or walking around, when they should be hunkered down in a protected concrete building. Some get killed by falling trees or hot wires. Some have been smacked by flying coconuts going about 100 MPH. You don't survive those accidents. Recovery efforts don't start until it's safe. Some of the typhoons play dirty tricks like blowing off the islands and heading north, and then doing a u-turn and coming right back after the people thought they were safe. Mother Nature is often unpredictable and unforgiving."

"How was last season? The hotel sits on a bluff and probably gets hit hard."

Horoto said, "The hotel was built to be almost typhoon resistant. You've probably noticed that the shutters going up and anything that is loose is being tied down. The maintenance guys know what they're doing. Last year, there were fourteen tropical storms and four typhoons in our islands. But those conditions don't always hit us direct, and sometimes they veer off and go north."

Johnny inquired, "So where do they go before they dissipate? Like when they hit land?"

"China, Philippines, Viet Nam, Taiwan and Japan get hit hard. The deadliest typhoon, Nina, smashed against China in 1975 and over 100,000 people were killed when the up-river dams burst. Taiwan has recorded the wettest typhoon ever in history but their run-off water system worked fine.

In eight hours, Typhoon Gertrude was blasting into Saipan at about 80 MPH, not reaching the super typhoon status. Johnny and Horoto has made sure that their guests were safely ensconced in their rooms, and he had earlier given his staff the option of returning to their homes, or having their families come to the hotel to be safe. Most elected to come to the hotel because they lived in ramshackle houses made of wood, tin and plywood, most of which could easily blow away. Guangman and his crew had prepared plenty of rice and sandwiches, enough for a three day retreat. Every room had several five-gallon bottles of water. The maintenance guys and Guangman's Korean staff had saved a few bottles each of the special Korean liquor, *sogu*, as he said "for the long black nights."

Each room had plenty of candles and flashlights. It was expected that the island power supply would be kaput and the hotel generator wouldn't be functional during the storm's highest velocity.

As the storm initially hit, island residents tried to register into the hotels for safety reasons. Soon the rooms were full, and many of the people offered to double-bunk, knowing full well that the entire population was enduring the raging storm as a group, and survival depended on them working together. Being hoi polloi, mucky-muck or filthy rich doesn't matter in real life and death matters.

Johnny was ecstatic about one special request—Jan Nan asked if she might stay with him in his protected quarters. For the next two days the storm roared and shook the buildings. The hotel was well-built. Those days for Johnny were memorable as he and Jan Nan lived by candlelight, made love and drank fine wine from Spain. It was almost disappointing that the storm was moving north.

On the third day, people began to crawl out from their safe quarters, and saw what the storm had wrought. It was actually humorous, however frightening, to see a palm tree naked without one frond remaining. The maintenance guys got the generator going, and soon Guangman was back at creating great meals and cinnamon rolls. His kitchen and restaurant had survived. Seuchill put a hand-written sign over the door, which said, "Go Forth and Feast." Guangman was back in business.

The grounds were cleaned up and most of the hotel guests headed home to see what was left of their homes. To pay for their keep, many of the younger local guests pitched in and helped to get the hotel back in good shape. The tourists now had a story that could be told and retold, and embellished at will about surviving the destructive tropical winds, and how the giant waves almost eroded the bluff at their hotel.

Johnny checked in with Tom and Carlos, and discovered except for a few broken windows, the Beach Hotel was doing fine. Their hotel was located right on the beach, and some of their shade huts, plants and decorations had been carried away by 10-foot breakers to ports unknown. Parts of their sandy beach had diminished but other parts had been built up.—so it was a trade-off.

Johnny asked, "When can you go back to work on some of the missing folks?"

"Give me a week or so to get back on track. We still have to find the Thompsons and figure out what the Yakuza is up to."

"The Yakuza part should be interesting, especially for me, the computer nerd."

Carlos laughed and said, "We might even get you a tattoo."

"That's okay, but leave my fingers alone. I need all of them for the keyboard."

Chapter 32

THE THOMPSONS UNEARTHED

Sooner than expected, Carlos called Johnny and said, "Saddle up. The Thompsons have been found. They showed up in a creek bed that fed into the lagoon. The heavy rain probably washed them out of their shallow grave from up above the arroyo."

"Who's at the crime scene?"

"Our favorite lieutenant, the Felix jerkoff. He got the area cordoned off with yellow barricade tape. He wouldn't let me get close. He threatened to arrest me again."

Johnny asked, "Did you call Dan? Maybe he can nose in and tell us what's going on."

"Yeah, I've got a call into his office. But the jurisdiction on this one is a little hazy and different. The Thompsons are American citizens, and do not fall into any international category. It's a little difficult for the FBI to get involved since it's not federal."

"Or if we can substantiate dope sales across state lines."

Carlos added, "Once we get hold of Dan, maybe he can come up with something. The lieutenant is acting his normal stupid self—no cooperation and coordination from that fool."

Johnny said, "Ever think Felix is dumb like a fox—like he's trying to throw us off the scent? Diversion and change of focus is often used in war and business, and possibly crooked cops."

"Time will tell the story on that one. He's the very definition of malevolent. Right now I think he's just a total jerk."

Johnny drove to the scene at the bottom of Suicide Cliff. This is the location in 1944 where hundreds of Japanese soldiers and families jumped to their deaths rather than surrender. They had been ordered by the Japanese Emperor to fight to their last breath but when backed up to the edge by the US Marines, they elected to jump rather than face disgrace.

As he drove up, Johnny saw Carlos and Dan talking, and then Dan moved up the ravine to the found body site. Johnny said, "What's Dan think?"

"He's going to talk to the lieutenant and see what they can work out. The Thompsons have been involved in drugs before, and had been known to move drugs back and forth by from state to state."

About a half-hour later, Dan met with Carlos and Johnny. He didn't look too happy and was red in the face. He said, "The fool continues to be belligerent and uncooperative. The bodies are relatively good shape—I took a few photos with my telephone. On a quick glance, it looked like they had been shot in the head. The man's pockets on his short had been turned out. Chances are that the cops did this—the pockets were still white inside. The whole crime scene is liable to erased before other detectives can get a thorough look, and of course, the general area will all be contaminated even before the ME gets there. About six people are tramping back and forth."

Carlos asked, "Did anyone go upstream to find the actual grave site? Might be some type of evidence in the hole."

Dan answered, "Felix said he sent two guys up the arroyo. He said they were newbies but were in better shape to walk up and cross the boulders in the creek bed."

Carlos said, "This gets crazier and crazier. There is no hurry on any of this and it's still daylight. Maybe Johnny is right that they are purposely screwing up all the investigations."

The ME, one of Carlos' old compadres, arrived and took control of the bodies. As he was loading the body bags into his pick-up truck, Carlos asked him if he noticed anything important or peculiar. The ME answered that they looked a typical healthy couple in their thirties, and it appeared that they had both been shot. He said he would know the caliber once he started the autopsy.

The ME did notice that a wristwatch had apparently been removed from the man. The body was covered with dirt and mud, except there was a clean circle around the man's right wrist.

Carlos asked, "Anything else?"

The ME answered, "The crime scene area where the bodies were found was covered with footprints, and everything around the bodies had been trampled. It almost seemed like it was done on purpose. But between you and me, most of the lieutenant's crime scenes are messed up. He's either incompetent or covering for someone. I've noticed this about him, case after case."

About a week later, the autopsy was as expected—bullets holes to the back of their necks, but two different calibers, a .38 round nose bullet, and a .40 hollow-nose slug. The man and woman were likely in a kneeling position and wondering what to expect, when the two slugs exoded in their brains and sent them off into oblivion. The man also several slugs in his torso, and some abrasions on his back. He must have fought his assailants.

During this time frame, two more female tourists had been assaulted—one at the American Memorial Park and another in downtown Garapan. The victims were getting more protective of their belongings and fought with their assailants. These confrontations ended up with both victims being injured and having to be treated at the Hospital ER. A Japanese victim had her arm run over by a getaway sedan.

Depressing news for the tour agencies and hotels. The government took these assaults in stride as just routine to the agencies. The PR people and police didn't organize any safety campaigns or develop citizen organizations, as eyes and ears only, to patrol the areas with radios to notify the police in case they saw something suspicious.

Some of the local population seemed intent on destroying their last viable island industry. The Russia tourist agencies ran a film for potential tourists showing a woman being attacked by a masked man wielding a knife. In the film, the assailant threatens the woman by pushing a knife against her ribs, and then pushing her out onto the asphalt roadway. Fortunately, she wasn't killed or seriously injured, ending up with scrapes and bruises.

Seuchill thought to herself, "Why would a tourist want to come to a dangerous island, when she could go Macau or Singapore?"

It was likely other lady tourists were thinking the same way.

Chapter 33

DEALING WITH THE YAKUZA

Horoto came bounding into the restaurant at the Californian and noticed Johnny sitting with Jan Nan at one of the view tables. They were holding hands across the table.

Horoto walked over to the table and said, "I hate to bust up this romantic interlude, but guess what?"

Johnny said, "I'm never any good at those guessing games. However, it must be good—you look excited and about ready to burst open with your info."

Horoto nodded a greeting towards Jan Nan. He said, "Should I continue?"

Johnny declared, "Sure, Horoto. No problem. Jan Nan is my lawyer and is sworn to secrecy and attorney—client privilege." He paused, "Wanna know something else?"

"Sure, but let me tell you the news first."

Johnny smiled and patted Jan Nan's engagement finger. Horoto didn't notice. He said, "I just spotted your favorite lieutenant, Felix, having lunch with three Yakuza members at the Hyatt Hotel. They seemed very buddy-buddy."

"Now that's interesting. What's Felix doing with high-power organized crime?"

"Damn good question!"

Johnny lifted up Jan Nan's arm and hand, and put the ring right in front of Horoto. He said, "Notice anything now?"

"Does that mean what I think it means? Are you engaged?"

Jan Nan and Johnny both smiled, and Johnny said, "Yep, it's for real."

"Congratulations. I'm happy for you guys. You make a great couple."

Johnny said, "Thanks, Horoto-san." He then asked, "Also, did Bobo tell you about the Yakuza party last night at the nearby Riko Hotel? There were about a dozen of the gangsters and about fifty girls on parade."

Horoto answered, "No, what was that about?"

"Tom and I figured it was an orientation part of veteran members being introduced to Saipan and its special 'attractions.' The girls were immaculately dressed in long gowns. Absolutely beautiful women—makeup perfect. There were also several Caucasian ladies."

"What happened? I didn't hear about any trouble."

"There wasn't any trouble. Each gang member picked out two girls that he liked, and they went off to dinner. *Menage a trois* was on the dessert menu. After the meal and a little island music and dancing, the men took the women to their rooms, and the ladies stayed the night."

Horoto asked, "The ladies left in the morning?"

Johnny said, "Bobo heard that the ladies left right after breakfast, and most of the Yakuza men flew back to Japan." He added, "I'll let Carlos and Dan know. Felix might be part of the Yakuza mob trying to spread their criminal web into Guam and Saipan. Carlos told me yesterday that there are two more people that have disappeared on Guam, and they were both in the dope-selling business."

Johnny said goodbye to Jan Nan, and was blessed with her concerned admonition, "Be careful. The Yakuza are every bit as violent as the Chinese tongs." Johnny had never experienced someone caring strongly about him since his mother held him in her arms.

Later in the day, Dan and Carlos met with the three Yakuza members at the Hyatt over appetizers and tropical drinks. The three had all the markings of true-to-life of authentic members and were not wanna-bees. Carlos made the introductions—Horoto had come along to serve as an interpreter. One of the men, the oldest with the most tattoos, spoke passable English, and had apparently been assigned to

Las Vegas for several years. The men were identified as Tosiwo Suzuki, Miko Hoshimo and Masao Hirhoki. None of the three were hesitant to identify themselves. They readily showed their Japanese passports.

After introductions, Dan asked what they were doing on Saipan.

Tosiwo answered in English after explaining the question to his fellow gangsters. Horoto had told Dan and Carlos that he would remain quiet unless the info was not being translated back and forth accurately. Dan looks over at Horoto whose nod meant yes.

Tosiwo said that they were vacation and enjoying the fresh air and the beautiful Chinese girls. Dan asked if he knew Felix, a local policeman. Tosiwo said that he had known Felix for several years. He added that about four years ago, his rental car had been stolen and Felix offered to get it back for a price. He said the car contained his passport and his snorkeling gear.

One day later, Felix returned the car and belongings for a one hundred dollars reward. Tosiwo added, "Since then, we always stay in contact with Felix. He's very good about arranging whatever we need, sometimes a girl or a secret place to gamble. For the men that like to smoke marijuana, Felix always has a dealer drop by the hotel."

Carlos thought to himself, "This Felix is as good as Bobo for arranging "things."

Dan asked, "Weren't you afraid that you get arrested for some of the illegal stuff?"

"No, never. Felix said he had everything under control. One of his favorite remarks was 'Don't worry. The other cops always do what I tell them.' Like today, do I have to give you money?" Under the table, he opened his leather bag and removed a thick wad of American hundred-dollar bills.

Dan smiled, "It doesn't work that way with the federal officers."

Tosiwo smiled back and said, "Then maybe we should stop talking. It's too nice a day to go to jail."

Dan asserted, "Now that we know each other, I'll just tell you that I don't care about this small stuff. However, if you're thinking about moving big-scale dope operations to Guam and Saipan, I can't let it happen. The federal agencies are on you, right from customs and immigration, to the FBI and the ATF."

Tosiwo said, "You Americans love acronyms and alphabet soup. The island operations are really too small to be profitable. There are not enough people."

Carlos said, "If that's the case, you have to stop killing off the small operators. We keep finding buried bodies on Saipan and Guam. It seems that there's a lot of weird stuff happening, like a battle over turf."

Tosiwo eyes twinkled and almost closed, "We didn't kill anyone. Maybe those dead people had nasty personalities. Maybe it had nothing to do with drugs?"

Carlos added, "It's all about drugs, hard stuff like heroin, cocaine, and ice. Marijuana is easy to grow and find, but maybe shipments are needed for Japan."

Tosiwo replied, "Drugs are dangerous business in Japan. The youth gangs are driving the Japanese authorities to come down hard on drugs users and sellers. The gangs are uncontrollable and typically look for quick yen and fancy cars. They also dress the part like wild non-matching clothing and watch hip-hop television with psycho dancing. They're like copycat gang-bangers."

"And what does that mean for you?"

"Yakuza had been around for five hundred years and has mostly gone legitimate. There's still a little activity past the gray of right and wrong, but violence is not usually necessary. Just the word 'Yakuza' puts people in the cooperative fame of mind."

Carlos smiled and asked, "Are you still into the drugs, and violence if necessary? You didn't answer my question before."

Tosiwo said, "No more questions now. My mind is "busy" with all the translating. My last line is 'we are here on vacation and for pleasure.' We are done with lunch. Hai." The three men got up and bowed. Horoto's bow was very deep. As the three men left, they paid for the food and drinks. They never looked back—not even a glance.

Carlos asked Horoto if Tosiwo had translated correctly. He said, "Most of the time. Tosiwo told the other two not to talk, but just to listen. You might have noticed that their faces were tighter than granite. No expression of any kind."

Dan said, "We just got jurisdiction over our favorite lieutenant. Sounds like he's not only corrupt and stupid, but also a pimp for the

Chinese girls. That is definitely FBI jurisdiction over cops abusing their power and authority. What a loser!"

Carlos said, "Sure explains the screw-ups at crime scenes, and being so low that he would steal a watch from a dead man."

Dan added, "We've got Tosiwo for bribery also. The problem with bending or twisting him a bit is that he will never talk."

Horoto asserted, "Even water-boarding won't work with the Yakuza, They would die first before turning their colleagues over to the police. They exposed Felix only because he is not a member and they have no respect for him. They, too, consider him a loser—just someone to use for their convenience."

Horoto asked, "What's next? More work?"

Carlos said, "Boo to work. Tom Parker has all the harnesses repaired on the sailboards. The breeze is about right. Let's go skimming across the lagoon."

Horoto replied, "I have work to do at the hotel."

Johnny said, "That work will wait. I got up on the boards last week. You can do it—I know."

With just a little hesitation, Horoto asserted, "Okay, I'll try. If I get killed, you will have a hard time finding a replacement."

Johnny said, "Awww, not so. We'll just hire a Yakuza guy. He'll know how to keep Bobo under control."

And off they went to the Beach Hotel's long sandy beach. Cocina, Daisy and Jan Nan were already there, munching fruit snacks and drinking cold sangria wine filled with tropical fruits. They were sitting under the newly built shade shelter with the palm fronds roof providing shade and protection from the tropical downpours. They looked mighty fine in their brightly-colored bikinis. It promised to be a wonderful, action-filled day of tanning and burning up of excess calories—another moment in time of exploring, dawdling and daydreaming.

How could such serenity and beauty be suspect or allow any evil to develop?

The children were whooping and hollering—not a care in the world. It was also good for the adults to play and be free.

Horoto got up on the board on his first try. We all heard his, "Woo-ooh!"

Chapter 34

FELIX'S CONFESSION

The frantic call came in the middle of the night. It was the obnoxious police lieutenant. Felix was begging for help. He added that a hit man was trying to kill him. He had barely escaped and was hiding in the jungle.

Carlos asked, "Why call me? Talk to your police buddies."

"Most of the guys are upset with me. They might not help; maybe just turn me over to the hit man for money."

Carlos asked, "Then, back to me. You know what I think of you, especially dealing with the Yakuza and turning your back on the police oath."

"What do you know about me? Do you know everything?"

"The Yakuza laid you out big-time."

Felix pleaded, "Please come to me. Bring your guns and maybe the FBI."

"Sounds like an ambush to me. Why should I take a chance?"

"No, I guarantee you. It's not an ambush. I need help before the bastard gets me." His cell phone started to go dead.

"Okay, where are you? What's the hit man look like."

"I'm behind the big water tank in Papago. The hit man is an ordinary-looking Asian guy, Japanese I suppose."

"Okay, I'll round up Dan. You stay low and if it's a set-up, you'll be the first one to die. Got it?"

"Yeah, please hurry. I'll tell you everything."

Carlos got Dan on the phone and they agreed to meet in the village of San Vicente. Three other agents showed up but Carlos and Dan felt that a low-profile entry would be the way to go. The Special Shooting Team on Guam was put on standby at the heliport of Anderson Air Force Base. Dan and Carlos drove Carlos' old non-descript Toyota. It could blend in anywhere on the island.

Within ten minutes, they were at the water tank. They turned off the motor, and sat and listened. The other agents were slowly moving towards the location.

A voice sounded, "I'm over here. Who's there?"

Carlos replied, "It's us. The whole area is surrounded by FBI agents and a helicopter is hovering over head."

Dan whispered to Carlos, "It sounds like Felix. But we don't who's in the bushes with him."

Carlos yelled, "Come out and show yourself. Any funny business, you'll be the first to drop."

"I'm alone. I don't know where the shooter is."

Carlos stepped out from the bushes, and Carlos turned the truck's headlights on him. He was unarmed and held his hands high in the air.

A rifle shot rang out from across the road, and a sedan sped out away from the water tank. Dan advised the other agents by radio, and they were right on the tail of the speeding sedan. Some people are born lucky. The shot clipped Felix in the arm at the same level as his heart. Six inches to his left, the bullet would have killed him instantly.

Dan and Carlos could hear the two vehicles roaring and screeching through the mountain passes. Carlos used an old towel as a compress on Felix's arm and told him to sit in the back of the truck. Carlos said, "Hang on. If you try to escape, we'll sic the local cops on your butt."

Dan added, "We'll also send Zeus."

Within minutes, they heard a terrifying crash, like something hit a non-moveable object. Carlos was hoping it was the bad guy. The shooter didn't know the roads and what areas were particularly slick. It had rained a half-hour before. Carlos called for an ambulance.

When Dan and Carlos reached the scene, a blue sedan was crushed against a telephone pole. The three agents were safe and had recovered an AK-47 and a Colt semi-auto pistol from the wreck. The driver was hanging onto life but not doing real well. There was no where to apply a tourniquet. He had massive head injuries and was likely suffering from internal bleeding. Apparently he hadn't been wearing a seat belt and took the steering wheel full in the chest. The car apparently didn't have an airbag, or hadn't deployed. The man looked Japanese, about forty years old, and had a few tattoos on his neck and torso.

The man tried to talk but it was a confusing language smeared with blood and spittle, but probably Japanese. His eyes were pleading for help but before the ambulance arrived, the light of life disappeared and he was dead. The night was quiet—no other sounds, except for the siren far in the distance that was likely the ambulance. Carlos got on the radio and advised the ambulance not to hurry—no need for another casualty.

Dan put Felix in the FBI tinted SUV, and told him to be quiet. The ambulance arrived and maneuvered the dead shooter's body out of the wreck. A traffic investigator showed up twenty minutes later, and Dan explained how he had come across the wreck while he going on an early morning hike. The officer looked skeptical but kept writing. Dan and Carlos followed the SUV to the FBI headquarters, where there was a temporary holding cell for prisoners.

Felix was cooperative and just happy to be alive. It's always the way with criminals and bullies, they are elated when they survive and seldom think of the harm and pain that they have caused others. Dan called a doctor friend of his, and the doctor said that Felix's injury was very minor. He gave him a tetanus shot and dressed the slight wound.

One of Dan's fellow agents checked the airport, and learned that the three Yakuza men from the Hyatt Hotel had already returned to Japan. The shooter had come in the day before, probably getting directions to take out Felix and how he operated. In the vernacular, he was a loose cannon and could cause irreparable damage to the organization.

Carlos made a large pot of coffee, and said to Felix, "It's going to be long night. So let's get started."

Felix said, "Got any cigarettes. I need a nicotine fix."

Carlos laughed and said, "Good luck with that one. No one smokes here."

Dan advised him of his Miranda rights, and asked if he wanted to talk without a lawyer present. Felix agreed to move on.

Dan said, "How did the shooter almost get you tonight?"

Felix answered, "Let's backtrack a bit. The money was coming too easy, so I figured I could get more out the Yakuza guys at the hotel. I told them I wanted more "consideration" or I would mention how the missing people were killed on Guam and Saipan."

Carlos asked, "You did the killing?"

"No, I just set up the shooters where to find the people and what their habits were."

Dan added, "Then you helped bury them?"

"Yeah, for extra money."

Dan asked, "Does that cover the missing Chinese couple and the Thompsons from the Californian Hotel."

Felix said, "Yeah, both. There's more to the story with the Thompson man. They used two shooters on this couple, because the man was so big and powerful. He resisted and they both shot him. But he carried a large Bowie knife and he managed to kill one of the shooters before he dropped dead. They must have shot him three of four times, including a head shot."

"Where's the knife now? They gave to me and I buried it with the Thompsons. On the crime scene where you saw me that day with the bodies, I had already found the knife and threw it in my duffle bag."

"Do you still have it? I want it to substantiate your story."

"Sure thing, it's at my house."

"May we voluntarily search your house, or should we get a court warrant?"

"Go ahead and search. I going to clean up this whole mess. I was a good cop before I started down the crooked road into easy money and gambling, and women besides my wife."

Dan said, "Okay now, we've determined the Yakuza is mad at you, and the shooter came after you. What happened?"

"It's as simple as this. My wife had left me and there was only me and three dogs at the house. Those dogs saved me. I can tell by their barks if they're hungry, excited, or there's a stranger coming into the yard. Being Japanese and not used to dogs, the shooter didn't expect such a noisy reception."

He continued, "I heard the low-growl barks, meaning there was danger in the yard. I had anticipated that the Yakuza might send a hit man, so I hightailed it out the bedroom window. As I jumped the perimeter fence into the jungle, two shots went whizzing over my head. The shooter didn't know the jungle trails like I did and I was soon over the hill and up to the water tank area. I heard him starting up his sedan, and knew that he would be patrolling the back roads looking for me. Fortunately I had grabbed my cell phone off the charger, so I was able to call you."

Carlos asked, "Now, on the Thompson case, where is the Yakuza's dead body? That one hasn't turned up.

"I was pretty drunk that night, and even when I was sober, I couldn't remember clearly where the body was buried. I think it was in the Cowtown area but I haven't been able to find it."

"Where are the guns they used? Nothing like that has been turned in, right."

"They gave them to me and told me to ditch them. I threw all the bullets off into the jungle and after I buried the Yukuza body, I threw the guns in the bay below Cowtown. That area has been hit by several big storms, so the guns may have washed out to the open sea."

Carlos asked, "They're not at your house?"

"No way. It's one thing to explain a knife but tougher than hell to explain the guns, especially if the bullets from the ME matched up with guns in my possession."

Straight on, Carlos asked, "Did you kill the Russian jogger, Nadena Romanoff?"

It was obvious from Felix's response, that he had never expected someone to tie him into this murder. He was thinking he was only looking at being an accessory to a murder by pointing out people and burying their bodies. This put on a whole different light on his confessions.

He responded, "Let me think about this for a minute."

Dan lambasted him with facts, "While keep in mind that we got DNA sample from the semen on and in her body, and also we can get a court order to have you tested. You know they're going to match."

"No, no, it wasn't me. I just found the body and buried it like the others."

"Believe what you want. We're going to hang this one on you, or you can keep coming clean, and let the court take your cooperation into consideration. Up to you."

He asked, "Where are you going to put me in jail? The corrections officers in our jails hate me, and the prisoners in there will wanna to do a number on me. I'm really scared about going to jail."

Carlos thought to himself, "Again the whimpering scumbag who had harmed dozens of other people, and killed a young woman just out exercising."

Dan asked, "Are you going to talk about it, or should we head over to the jail and book you in?"

"Okay, I'll talk about it."

"You want a lawyer or not? I don't wanna hear you in court complaining that we violated your Constitutional Rights." He looked over at Carlos and said, "Carlos, please turn on the tape recorder. I want to make sure about this."

Dan went through a litany of rights and got approval by Felix that he knew it was being recorded and that he wanted to talk about the case.

Carlos asked again, "Did you kill the Russian jogger." He set the time and date for the recording.

Felix answered, "I killed her. It was all a big mistake. My wife had left me and I wanted some sexual excitement. At first, she played along. But when I entered her, she tried to stop me. There was big rock near our blanket, and I hit her hard on the side of her head. She fainted and I finished until I climaxed. A few minutes, I tried to revive her, but she was dead. So I buried her. You know the rest of the story. You guys found her and dug her up."

Dan asked, "Anything else?"

He answered, "No, nothing. I didn't mean to kill her. I had been drinking. That's a problem for me. Can you put me in some other jail besides our jail in Susupe?"

Dan said, "We'll keep you here until we can transport you over to the Guam jail. They have some segregation cells that will keep you away from the other prisoners."

Carlos thought, "Here he goes again. Trying to excuse his behavior on alcohol—what a BS artist!"

Dan arranged for an Air Force chopper to pick him up, and he rode along until Felix was safely in the Guam jailhouse. He would deliver the court order for a DNA sample in a few weeks. The sample on the jogger's body had deteriorated but was still strong to retrieve a valuable sample.

Dan served a search warrant on Felix's house. The knife was retrieved and excellent DNA samples were recovered. The hit men's guns were not in the house or buried in the yard.

Chapter 35

FINDING THE LAST BODY

Carlos and Johnny were determined to find the missing Yakuza hit man's body. Most of the killings and burials had been in the general vicinity of Marpi and Cowtown on the northern end of the island. Most of the land there is public and there's still a lot of deep virgin jungle. Again, Carlos realized there would have to be roads to the general dump area. Murders and body dumps had been committed in this area long before Tom, Carlos, Johnny and Horoto had arrived on island. It was a piece of the island that had seen long, bitter struggles between the American Marines and the Japanese Imperial Army. Old soldiers' bones were still occasionally dug up, and also some of the ancient Chamorro warrior camps had been found on the land.

Bodies can last a long time on the island; mainly it is an island without predators, except for humongous rats that had been hidden in cargo, or boonie mongrel dogs and feral cats that had been brought in by the Spanish and privateers. There are no owls or hawks, and even sea gulls which clean up beaches all over the world. Except for a few rooting pigs and curious doves and pigeons, buried bodies are left alone, except for the usual insect infestations.

For the first several weekends, Carlos took out Zeus and some of his mongrel pals on the hunt. They had been successful in finding the Russian jogger but no luck this time. Felix hadn't been able to provide any more info except he had buried the Yakuza hit man in the Cowtown area. He was still using "the drunken defense" in all of his statements.

The guns that he had thrown in the ocean had not shown up in the deep sand and rocks, and Carlos and Johnny had walked the beach area a dozen times. Several of Carlos' friends went diving and snorkeling along the shoreline—again with negative results. The way the tides work in that area, the guns could have been carried many miles away or fell deep into the Marianas Trench (the deepest depth of all of the oceans in the world).

Carlos was not to be discouraged. He took on the burial find as a personal mission. He went to the pet stores and clubs, and worked out a search pattern with dozens of dogs on the hunt for the burial site. Everyone enjoyed being involved, and probably the dogs more than the humans. It was a big party for them, getting to run free in the jungle and having great snacks afterwards.

More wartime bones were found, and some old canteens and rifle cartridges. The find of the day was an old military Japanese rifle which took its place in a prominent showcase in the American Memorial Wartime Museum.

On one rainy day, the turn-out was less than than an average sunny, pleasant day. The wind was blowing hard and the rain occasionally coming down in sheets. It was a good time to find items that get turned up by rain and flowing waters like graves and ancient items, or maybe Spanish treasure.

Carlos let out a yelp first thing in the morning. He had found a Chamorro oval-shaped throwing stone. The children gathered around in a lean-to out of the rain to take a look and feel the polished roundness of the stone. As his Chamorro grandfather had told him, Carlos explained that ancient Chamorros didn't use bow and arrows and swords. Their weapon of choice was throwing rocks which weren't very effective for longer distances. So the weapon makers designed a sling apparatus which could project the stone effectively up to one hundred yards. The sling stones were mainly usually for tribal warfare, and some times for fishing in shallow waters. The stones are now found in the most unlikely of places because as with any weapon, there are often misses and the stones ended up deep in the jungles; and to be found later after rainstorms.

The following weekend, Carlos organized one hundred dogs and masters. It was quite the sight to see all the mixes, colors and ages of the dogs. The mutts were romping in the grass and chasing each around trees and stumps, playing some kind of game that humans could never understand. It appeared like "a dog park" in an urban setting, but in this case there were no fences or boundaries.

Carlos organized long lines walking side-by-side and within an hour, Zeus let out a loud bark. Carlos recognized this level of bark, not warning or fear, but outright excitement. The other dogs gathered around him, barking and milling about.

Carlos checked the area and saw that the ground was slightly lower. It was mushy and muddy. Carlos had several of the dog owners hold the dogs back and he started a dig with the small shovel from his pack. After a few digs, he struck something hard, brushed away the dirt, and saw that a skull was peering through the debris. Several of the children screamed. The grave had been found. Now it had to be determined that indeed it was the Yakuza hit man.

The dogs and masters were told that they could go home if they wanted to or stay and watch but out of the way of the ME's work. A television crew showed up, as well as reporters for the newspapers.

The ME was called. He showed up with a digging crew and went to work. Right away, the ME indicated that to Carlos that the man was a local islander and not Japanese and he was old, older than the Yakuza man. Carlos said, "OMG, another island mystery. The tiny island has been called 'Prostitution Island' and 'Gambling Island,' and now the islanders might be looking at a new title of 'Murder Island.' Sure were a lot of buried bodies for a small island. The autopsy should let us know what happened with this guy."

The ME said, "I'll keep you posted. He might also match up with the other missing cases like a husband or boyfriend."

As the workers loaded the victim into a body bag, the ME said, "I don't see any obvious injuries or trauma to this guy. Maybe it's a natural and the family just buried him out here in the wilderness. That's the way it was done in the old days."

Carlos said, "Looks like we keep looking for our Yakuza hit man." He notified the dog masters that were left about the ME's initial findings, and they all agreed to meet up again the following Sunday.

The ME called Carlos three days later, and said the old man had a note in his pocket identifying him as Tomas Marquez, a longtime resident from Chuuk. He added, "We contacted his wife, and there is an official death certificate indicating death by 'natural causes.' She said that he had died at home, and they had no money to bury him, so his sons took him to a nice place near a ridge overlooking the ocean. I told her now there was public cemetery where they could bury him gratis. The sons are going to build him a plywood box for his eternal rest."

Carlos said, "Looks like we continue our quest next weekend."

The ME jokingly commented, "Hey, give me a call when you find your guy. I'm always looking for new clients, and what's nice about my clientele, they never complain about the hardness of their beds or the room temperature, probably unlike the hotel business."

Carlos laughed and said, "Yeah, but my clients are more fun to talk to. I'll keep you posted on new customers."

The search continued as planned for the following weekend. This time, there were 110 dogs, all barking and sniffing, and raring to go to work. No luck again.

The next weekend, things were about to change. Alpha dog Zeus let out a loud bark, deeper and longer than before. When the handlers got close, they saw about twenty dogs barking and howling. Carlos said, "All that racket means more than a small shrew or ugly rat. Zeus' bark is one of excitement and determination. It means we found the grave—I can feel it."

The dogs had already dug into the makeshift grave, and already an arm was showing. It was tattooed. The handlers held the dogs back but it took a strong man to keep Zeus at bay. Zeus had found and wasn't about to let his quarry get away. After Carlos called the ME, he took a dozen photos with his telephone.

The ME and his crew showed up about thirty minutes later. He smiled and said, "At least you let me have a weekend of rest." He asked, "Where's the grave?"

Carlos pointed to a spot about one hundred yards away. "This is probably the guy; plenty of tattoos. Some Yakuza markings"

After an hour of meticulous digging, the ME looked up from the digging site and said, "Looks like the missing Yakuza. Lots of tattoos and about the right age—Asian extraction. Some of his obvious wounds look like a knife attack. The knife cut and chipped into a lot of his bones."

"Good news, but we'll have to find another form of recreation for the mutts every weekend." He added, "Regarding the murder weapon, I believe the FBI has the knife with a DNA report; now it is just a matter of matching the DNA from the knife to the body."

The ME crew loaded up the body into a dark green body bag. The ME said, "I'll let you know what I find. No obvious ID on the man."

Two days later, the ME called and said, "It's as expected. The body matches the description from Felix, and he did die from knife wounds. The DNA has been matched with the dried blood found on the confiscated knife." He asked, "Do you suspect Felix might be the killer?"

"No, I think it happened as described by Felix in our interviews."

The ME said, "No ID on the victim. There have been no calls reporting a male missing Japanese. I'll let the Japanese consulate know, just in case someone decides to report this guy missing. We did a match-up of an unused ticket at Asiana Airlines—the passenger that never showed up was Hideo Nakayama."

"So much for the code of honor, and Yakuza members taking care of each other. He was just a tool used, an insignificant pawn, and now gone like he never existed."

The ME chuckled and added, "He likely knew the rules. Maybe someone, somewhere will light a candle in his memory . . . or maybe not."

Chapter 36

DECISION TIME—JAN NAN

Jan Nan and Johnny had spent almost a year together, and they were still in the lustful "can't keep my hands off of you" stage. Friends had told Johnny that love falls into three stages with some overlapping: the sexual excitement of the young, the habituation of the middle-aged and mutual dependence of the old. Johnny was ready to experience love at all levels and ages but there was a slight reluctance on Jan Nan's part.

It wasn't a money issue—they were set financially; nor was it immigration or uncertainty as to where each wanted to live in the marriage. Saipan was a good neutral zone between China and California. Jan Nan had already started the divorce from her Chinese husband which could be done right in the Saipan courts. But she had some family concerns in that it might affect her father as he had arranged the marriage. He said that he and her husband would both lose face in traditional China.

Johnny asked, "Is your husband willing to let your daughter, Sun Hee, come to you on Saipan?"

"Yes, not a problem. He wants what's best for her. He knows that she will have a good education and be fluent in the world's main languages, Chinese and English. She might follow in my footsteps in becoming a lawyer."

"Is that what she wants? She should have a big say in her future. We don't want you tagged as a Tiger Mom, even if it's intended for long-term success. I know I would be terrible trying to be a tough Dragon Dad."

Jan Nan frowned, "I'm not a Tiger Mom but I will insist that she work hard academically, but she will have playtime and a chance to visit her friends. She likes the violin and that might be her calling."

Johnny smiled, "I can't wait to hear her play. I've never had children so you will have to teach me along the way."

"Good. She'll be here in about two weeks. All the paperwork for her stay has been done."

Johnny asked, "So how we work through this issue of losing face? What's your husband say?"

"I told him that he was free to date other women and he kind of hinted that he had a girl friend from a nearby town. So I think that's a good sign that he might let me go without any animosity or hurt. He's a good man and I would like to stay friends with him, and he is Sun Hee's father."

"If your husband agrees, maybe he would call your father and let him know about the decision—that way he wouldn't lose face. He could always tell everyone that it was a mutual decision between you and your husband, with no hard feelings."

"Hey, you might be a good lawyer. I think that will be okay with my father."

One week later, it had been worked out with Jan Nan's husband and father. She was free to divorce.

Johnny got down on one knee and made his proposal of marriage and ever-lasting love. She accepted—they both knew she would. The divorce papers were signed the next day, and the wedding was planned a few weeks after Sun Lee's arrival from China. Jan Nan wanted her to get used to the idea of another man in her mother's life. Johnny's hotel apartment was large enough to accommodate his new family, and Sun Lee would end up with her own room with a television, air conditioner and plenty of closet space.

The wedding took place on the Sunset Cruise catamaran. It was one of those soft, balmy nights and the water was perfectly flat, appearing that you could walk across the sea to Tinian. The best man was Carlos and his wife Daisy was the maid of honor. Sun Hee was the flower girl and ring bearer combined. She couldn't stop smiling up at her mother. After the ceremony, she stayed the night with Carlos and Daisy, and their three adorable children.

The ceremony was performed by a local padre and it was short and to the point of the meaning of life together and the sanctity of the marriage vows. Johnny and Jan Nan meant every word, and they both teared up and smiled. It was a new beginning for Jan Nan and the start of a new intimate journey for Johnny.

A local cowboy band provided the music, and Dan Simpson joined in with his banjo. It was fun and festive. The band also knew reggae, and they did a dozen Bob Marley tunes. The bride and groom had changed into island aloha clothing, and their wedding dance was the hit of the evening.

As they left the boat, Carlos whispered to Johnny and Jan Nan, "My friends, live, love and proliferate. Go forth and grab a big hunk of life."

And that's what they did, ever after and forever.

Epilogue

Natural beauty and a carefree sort of life prevail on Saipan. It is blissful and blessed. Humans cannot screw it up, while many generations of Chamorros, Carolinians, Spanish, Germans, Bangladeshi, Filipinos and Americans have tried, not intending to, but just by their mere presence have put a strain on the ecosystem. The old-timers tell us that just 50-60 years ago, you could paddle out to the reef in the morning, and return before dark with a boatload of fish and crab. But now the fishermen have to venture out 50-100 miles to get a boatload, spend days on the sea, and pay a fortune for fuel.

Tourists have arrived and spent money, and increased the local family' level and style of living. When times were good, they bought new trucks and gold chains. They expected luxury and convenience, and now polluted water is flowing into the lagoon and beaches are being categorized as unsafe for human recreation. Islanders are experiencing high levels of diabetes and heart problems, as they consume a diet of processed meats and potato chips, and frequent fast food restaurants. There is always a clamor to go back to the "old ways,' and so they try to teach offspring how to traditionally dance and speak Chamorro or Carolinian . . . and to learn fishing and farming. But the kids are more interested in Lady Gaga and Ipad games, and fewer and fewer are learning the languages or developing an interest in the old island cultures.

There is an old saying about "how you keep them on the farm once they have seen Paris," and the same is true about the sleepy, laid-back island life. Many of the youngsters go off to college in California or Arizona, and most never come back. They enjoy the faster and more convenient life of the Mainland and besides there are fewer and fewer jobs on the home islands. If you're not connected politically and by family ties, your chances of landing a good job are just about nil. As one Criminal Justice graduate recently said, "I'm going to California—I have the wrong name ever to get a police or fire job on Saipan."

Conversely Saipan remains the perfect place once you have outgrown the Mainland, or are sick and tired of too much hassle and the intrigues and twisted values of the Washington political bullcrap. Here you can experience life at its basic level with food and shelter, and a chance to climb Maslow's pyramid of human progression right to self-actualization with art, music, writing and self-expression at your own speed. You will also find that you can travel through life in Micronesia without so much "stuff," material things that can just bog you down. Comedian George Carlin talked about life when he became philosophic, "Enjoy yourself all the time, and do whatever you want. Don't be seduced by that mindless chatter going around about 'responsibility.' That's exactly the sort of thing that can ruin your life . . . Trying to make something out of today only robs you of precious time that could be spent daydreaming or resting up." A good spot for that is on Lau Lau Beach on the Pacific Ocean side of Saipan.

Tom Parker and Carlos Montano enjoy and thrive on running their hotel on the beach, and also keeping up the high standards of Allan Pinkerton (1819-1884) and the "Private Eye' business. They're always snaring bad guys and serving papers on scoundrels. Their wives are magnificent in their understanding and support.

Johnny Ornelas and Yoshi Horoto have their hotel under control and are keeping the murders to a minimum. There are still spottings of ghosts and tao-taomonas but people have come to realize, although scary and frightening, there's nothing on the record that show these spiritual creatures hurt or maim. Anyway, its best that you're soused to fully experience their appearances, and there haven't been any extra-terrestrial green men noticed lately—even on those crystal clear nights with innumerable stars.

Bell Captain Bobo Camacho has become a model employee and is continually searching for ways to increase the patronage and profits of the hotel and restaurant. He realizes that he benefits also when receipts are high. Out of habit, Horoto keeps a close eye on Bobo. So far, no "sticky" fingers. Bobo has not taken on a new teenage mistress—maybe he is getting older and wiser.

Guangman and Seuchill are as reliable as ever—still turning out delicious meals and of course, hot steamy cinnamon rolls. The restaurant keeps thriving because the local people enjoy the fare as much as the tourists—Guangman started a "local Chamorro" night, and the tables are full until midnight. There's still sogu coming in from Korea, and delightful wines are available from the hills of the Philippines. And robust cigars too!

Han Gaozu and his entourage, with Simi holding a briefcase full of hundred-dollar bills, come back every six months, splitting their time between the hotels. When it's time to leave, the briefcase is empty. Maybe he isn't laundering money, but possibly just a lousy gambler from an affluent family.

On the islands, we just kind of flow through life like "fat, dumb and happy," but we're always ready for interesting things to happen. One day peacefully flows into the next.

The Mystery Hotel, legally known as **The Californian Hotel**, has rooms waiting for you. Everyone has a story—how about yours? The hotel hasn't had a guest murdered in over a year and it's believed to be relatively safe. Just watch out for dope dealers and tattooed men with missing fingers!

Willing to take a chance and book a room? VIP discounts are available!

Make a move—get off the freeway. Smell the torch ginger, protea, and night-blooming jasmine and enjoy the colors and textures of the gorgeous hibiscus, anthurium, and bougainvillea. Feel the smooth orchids. You won't be sorry . . . .

Post-Script—Whoops

Another year passed . . . and then the hotel had one of those "whoops" moments to add to the revival of the mystery factor. Things had been very peaceful and non-threatening on the premises and the beach until that lazy afternoon.

It was a typical tropical day with the soft tradewinds blowing across the grounds. The majority of the hotel guests were following their usual breakfast-lunch-snooze routine. Two guests were bird-watching and another was flat on his back with an electronic reader shading him from the sun.

A verbal alarm broke the calm. Bobo and the third floor housekeeper came urgently running into Johnny's office and Bobo exclaimed, "We've got a problem!" Horoto had seen the two running down the hallway and joined them in Johnny's office.

Johnny looked up from his computer screen and asked, "What's the problem? Slow down, so I can understand you."

Bobo took a deep breath and said, "It's Enrique Ramos, the man that has been with us for two months. He won't answer his door, and the safety catch is locked from inside." He looked at Helena, the housekeeper, and said, "Tell him what you told me."

Helena shyly said, "Yes, Senor. Usually Room 309 is one of the first rooms I clean right after lunch. But today when I went by, there was a hotel "Do Not Disturb" sign on the door knob. I could hear the stereo or television playing softly. So I moved right along and cleaned the nearby rooms. When I finished at about 3:35, the sign was still there. This was unusual for Mr. Ramos—he's usually out by the pool in the afternoon.

"I thought maybe Senor Ramos had forgotten to remove the sign, or was sick. I knocked twice on the door but there was no answer. I used my pass key but the door would only open a few inches and was secured by the inside security catch. I yelled inside but no answer. That's when I came and told Bobo."

Bobo added, "His Toyota Tundra is still in the parking lot."

Johnny and Horoto decided to take a look. Once upstairs, Johnny tried to push the door open but the security catch was strong and firm. He yelled inside to no avail. Horoto asked Bobo if there was another way into the room without damaging the door and frame. There wasn't an adjoining room door to open.

Bobo told Helena to find a "young" agile maintenance worker to climb up and go through the above sliding door. She found Robbie who went to the second floor balcony just below Room 309 and noticed a rope dangling over the side from the balcony above. He set his ladder and scrambled up to the next floor. The slider was open, and Robbie went inside, and let Johnny and Horoto in through the front door.

They didn't see Senor Ramos, but they noticed the bedroom door was askew. Johnny peeked inside and saw a naked Senor Ramos flat on his back with a nasty black knife in his chest. His penis had been sliced off. There was a full-figured Hawaiian woman slumped over a chair at the writing desk. She was wearing only a lava-lava skirt. She had begun to write a note—the lettering was erratic and nearly illegible. The note was covered with blood that had leaked from her nose.

Both victims were dead . . . very dead!

Helena exclaimed, "OMG, that's Rosie. She's a *puta!*"

Johnny looked over at Horoto and declared, "Time to call Carlos . . . again!"

Horoto said, "Hai. At least we had a couple of peaceful years . . ."

Quotations

(That Make You Think)

Albert Campus (1913-1960)—"Murder is terribly exhausting."

Ambrose Pierce—"There are three kinds of homicide: felonious, excusable, justifiable . . . and praiseworthy."

Chief Justice Earl Warren—"The crime problem is in part an overdue debt that the country must pay for ignoring for decades the conditions that breed lawlessness."

Daniel Webster (1782-1852)—"Every unpunished murder takes away something from the security of every man's life."

Friedrich Nietzsche (1844-1900)—"Distrust all men in whom the impulse to punish is powerful."

Gangster Al Capone—"You can get much farther with a kind word and a gun, than you can with a kind word alone."

George Carlin, Comedian (1937-2008)—"The keys to America: the cross, the brew, the dollar, and the gun."

Justice Louis D. Brandeis—"Crime in contagious. If the government becomes a lawbreaker, it breeds contempt for the law."

Lord Voldemort—"Get back here, Potter! I want to see your face when I kill you! I want see the light leave your eyes."

Mark Twain—Always do right. This will greatly gratify some people, and astonish the rest."

Mary Welsh Hemingway—"The ancient maxim has been confirmed many times, that to an appreciative audience, people delight in talking about themselves . . ."

Oscar Wilde—"Murder is always a mistake—one should never do anything one cannot talk about after dinner."

Peter Drucker—"We know nothing about motivation. All we can do is write books about it."

Shakespeare in *Hamlet*—"There is nothing good or bad, but thinking makes it so . . ."

Sir Thomas Browne (1605-1882)—"The long habit of living indisposeth us for dying."

Thomas Jefferson (1743-1826)—"If no action is to be deemed virtuous for which malice can imagine a sinister motive, then there never was virtuous action"

Thomas Mann—"A man's dying is more the survivor's affair than his own."

Ugo Betti—"Murderers, in general, are people who are consistent, people who are obsessed with the idea."

Rudyard Kipling, poet, (1865-1936)—"A woman is only a woman, but a good cigar is a smoke."

Oscar Wilde, writer, (1854-1900)—"Yet each man kills the thing he loves..."

T.R. Marshall, politician, (1854-1925)—"What this country needs is a good five-cent cigar."

Glossary

Au naturale—in the buff, naked (French)

Brujas—witches (Spanish, Filipino)

Bula-bula—BS, bogus, bragging

Coyote—guides, illegal runners for drugs and illegal immigrants (slang)

Guapo—handsome, good looking (Spanish, Filipino)

Ice—slang for illegal drug—amphetamines

Kama Sutra—an ancient Indian Hindu book about human sexual behavior

Lei—necklace of fresh flowers (Hawaiian)

Mahalo—thank you (Hawaiian)

Mangkukulam—a hovering ghost, usually under or near a palm tree (Filipino)

Masarap—delicious, tasty (Filipino)

ME—medical examiner, takes custody of body for autopsy

Mwar-mwar—a head crown of flowers (island of Pohnpei)

Nada—nothing, zilch, zip, wala (Spanish-Filipino)

Ohana—family (Hawaiian)

OMG—oh my gawd

Putas—whores, prostitutes, ladies of the night, poontang, pleasure women

Quid Pro Quo—Latin, meaning "what for what," tick for tack, etc.

Sakau—kava, mildly narcotic drink made from plants on Pohnpei

Tae Kwando—ancient Korean art of self-defense and human control

Tao-taomonas—spiritual beings, found in the jungle and dark places (Chamorro)

Tsismis—gossip (Filipino)

Voila—call to attention, magic, express approval (French)

WTF—what the frig? what's going on?

Yakuza—organized crime ring, often called Japanese Mafia